Purrfectly Mated

A MAVERICK PRIDE TALE

THE MAVERICK PRIDE TALES
BOOK ONE

C.D. GORRI

Purrfectly Mated:
A Maverick Pride Tale #1
by C.D. Gorri
Edited by BookNookNuts

Copyright 2019, 2022, NJ, C.D. Gorri

For all you Shifter lovers,
Your purrfect mate is out there.
Don't ever lose faith!
del mare alla stella,
C.D. Gorri

This is a work of fiction. All of the characters, names, places, organizations, and events portrayed in this novel are either part of the author's imagination and/or used fictitiously and are not to be construed as real. Any resemblance to any person, living or dead, actual events, locales or organizations is entirely coincidental. This eBook is licensed for your personal enjoyment only. All rights are reserved. No part of this book is to be reproduced, scanned, downloaded, printed, or distributed in any manner whatsoever without written permission from the author. Please do not participate in or encourage piracy of any materials in violation of the author's rights. Thank you for respecting the hard work of this author.

Blurb

He's the leader of his Pride. She's a normal with no idea Shifters exist.

Calling a Magical Matchmaking Service isn't exactly ideal, but Hunter Maverick is desperate to find his mate.

If he doesn't have control of the eight-hundred-pound Tiger living inside him, he can't run the Pride. The best way to manage his beast is to claim a female as his own, but no one in his Pride calls to him. Only his fated mate will do.

There's just one problem.

He has no idea who she is.

Elissa Phoenix has hit rock bottom. When she's cajoled into accepting a blind date, she finds herself in one lousy situation after another. Bad manners and lewd suggestions leave Elissa no choice but to leave on her own.

Stranded in the rain on the side of the road, Elissa is startled when an elderly stranger in a limo offers her a ride. She knows she should run, but her gut says get in. With no other prospects, what does she have to lose?

Uncle Uzzi has found the purrfect mate for the big bad Tiger of Maverick Point, New Jersey, wandering on the side of the road, but it's up to the growly Neta to win her heart.

Can Hunter convince Elissa she's his purrfect mate?

Welcome to Uncle Uzzi's Magical Matchmaking Service!

Uzzi Stregovich sat at his dining room table and perused the comic section of the Sunday paper with his usual steaming mug of black tea and a heaping plate of cookies beside it.

Richard, the housekeeper, came in once a week to keep the old Witch stocked, and his efforts were appreciated. His services had been a gift from Uzzi's beloved wife, Betty, when she'd been in hospice.

"You see, *liebling*, they still have *Dagwood* in the funnies during the holiday season," he mused aloud.

Humming to himself, Uzzi ignored the first tingle of awareness that buzzed along his skin. It was always that way when the Magic wanted his attention. For eighty-three years the Witch had been matching up supernatural pairs, and he was still going strong.

Though, to be fair, he had lost some *oompf* when his own beautiful wife had passed on to the next part of her existence.

Uzzi often got requests, but that was not the way his Magic worked. This was no on demand service. He wasn't *Netflix*, for pity's sake.

He was a Witch. A direct descendant of the Goddess of Love herself, in her many incarnations, truth be told. As such, he had special talents.

Finding fated mates and bringing them together, was of course more than a talent. It was a gift and a responsibility. After he found his own soul in his sweet Betty, he'd made a vow to help others. His wife had been all for it. She'd even designed his business cards.

Uncle Uzzi's Magical Matchmaking Service was happy to provide consultations. Of course, after he met with prospective clients, Uzzi's Magic was the final decision maker.

It chose whether or not to take on such and such as his next project. If a client was rejected, it was usually because the timing was not right. On rarer occasions, it was because that person did not have a fated mate. Sad for sure, but Uzzi knew better than to question the powers that be.

The Universe had its own ideas of who deserved a fated mate and when and where such mates should meet. Uzzi preferred to not work against such an ever present force. He was merely there to assist.

Working with the Fates, the Muses, and the Universe at large was always better for business, and for his clients. Harmony, balance, duty, honesty, and honor were tantamount in his business, and necessary for his Magic to work.

Magic had its own way of letting him know which clients to choose next, and since his skin was tingling right then, he knew. His next project was coming, and soon. Uzzi made a few calls, packed a bag, and then sat down to wait.

It wouldn't be long now.

Prologue

Uncle Uzzi logged onto his new laptop with a sparkle in his eye and winked at his dearly departed Betty's picture that he kept in a silver frame on his desk.

"Twenty years without you, love, and I still remember the day I took that picture, *liebling*," he whispered.

Being a male Witch, and the indirect-direct, depending on who was telling the story, descendant of the goddess of Love, Aphrodite herself, Uzzi had been gifted with many talents in his lifetime. Finding fated mates for supernaturals, including himself, was one of them.

If only Uzzi had known that he would have to live without his Betty for so long, he thought and shook his snowy white head. His locks were just as full and thick as when he'd been a young man, but instead of brown, they were white. His full beard, too.

"Someday, *liebling*, I will join you. At least I have my work," he said, and told Betty about his newest case.

The supernatural community had been contacting Uzzi Stregovich for years, hailing his Magical Matchmaking Services as the premier place to find a mate.

What could he say? He had a gift, and he insisted on sharing it with the world.

"Ah, here we are. Maverick Point, New Jersey. Ooh, I wonder if that is near the famous Bear Claw Bakery," he mused.

Uzzi scrolled through his email and clicked on the email he'd received. It seemed the Maverick Pride Neta needed help finding a mate. Now that was something Uzzi could do beyond a doubt. After another lengthy perusal over the message from the unfortunately mate-less Shifter, Uzzi felt his Magic spark and sizzle.

"Tiger, tiger, burning bright," he said aloud, and grinned at his own joke.

"Let's see, Maverick Point, yes, yes, I remember you," he told the email.

Grabbing a picture of his wife, he kissed the image and winked. His Betty always knew which matches were worth making. She was his whole heart, even more so now that was gone.

"Time to make another match, *liebling*. Come, let's go to work now," he told the photo, turning back to close his computer screen.

"And as for you, I shall see you soon, my boy. Leave it to Uncle Uzzi," he said, and clicked the power button.

Uzzi took his cell phone out and dialed the number to his favorite driving service and ordered a car to take him to the Jersey town that very night. When there was a mate to be found, time was precious.

"We are off, *liebling*. Time for some Magic," he said and pressed a kiss to his finger before touching the glass over her cheek.

His wife was always with him. She was his inspiration, and his compass, always pointing true.

Nothing could stop true love, he remembered her saying with a small smile.

It was a message he carried to all his clients, and

the Tigers of Maverick Point were about to find out what that meant, starting with the Neta.

Uzzi felt the Universe's approval in the air around him and in his Magic. It was time.

"Oh yes, Neta, you are going to meet your fated mate, and very soon."

Chapter One

How the fuck did I wind up here?

It was all Elissa could do not to slam her face down on the table as she pondered that question for the umpteenth time since leaving her cozy Hoboken apartment to go on this so called date.

"So, babe," the over-stuffed, heavily-cologned, and downright fugly man said.

Her date of the evening looked like something out of a bad sitcom as he tried to lean over the stained tablecloth of the rundown hotel buffet room, he'd driven two hours to get to. Waggling his caterpillar-like eyebrows, he gave her the once over and Elissa's skin crawled.

Oh, hell no.

"I got a room upstairs, you know, for *after*," he told her, nodding his head, and biting his lower lip in a manner she assumed he thought was provocative.

At best, it was nauseating.

FML.

How was this guy Elissa's date for the evening? What had she done to deserve this?

Little Gianni. Yup, that was how he'd introduced himself. And here she was. On a blind date with a guy who had the word 'little' in front of his name.

Well, what did she expect? Roses and champagne? In this economy? She didn't know where Cinder-fucking-ella got her prince, but it sure as fuck wasn't in Jersey.

Elissa could only blame herself for agreeing to go on this blind date. Initially, the whole Little Gianni fiasco had been intended for her roommate.

Wait a second. Scratch that thought.

It *was* all Gretchen's fault. That ungrateful cow!

She tried to play it off like she was some sweet little homegrown maiden. Oh, just wait till Elissa got home. Gretchen was never going to hear the end of it.

She owed Elissa. Big time. Like a whole month of

washing the dishes big time. The rat trap they shared in her hometown of Hoboken was all the two women could afford, and for the most part, they got along just fine.

In fact, they'd grown to be close friends over the three years they'd lived together. It was the only reason she'd ever agreed to this date from Hell.

Elissa sighed and looked over at Little Gianni. Maybe he wasn't all that bad?

"*BEEEELLLLLLLCHHH!* 'Scuse me, doll. Better out, am I right?"

Gianni winked and Elissa wished for a black hole to open up and swallow her up right through the floor.

OMFG.

The man just burped out loud like he was in a frat boy belching contest, only those days passed him up about thirty years ago.

For fuck's sake. Gretchen, you so owe me.

Elissa cursed her roommate and tried not to groan. But Little Gianni wasn't quite done. The grown ass man lifted his leg and let one rip.

Right. Fucking. There.

Elissa was going to die before the end of the night.

Literally.

This is what you get when you do a friend a favor without asking for details! Idiota!

The voice of her Italian grandmother sounded in her brain. She tried to ignore it, willing herself not to wince at the man while he sucked air, and who knows what else, noisily through his coffee-stained teeth.

Ew. So gross.

That was the perfect word to describe it. The only word, in fact. The entire date was just so fucking gross. She still couldn't believe her sweet little roommate from Iowa, *Gretchen Kaepernick*, she of the wispy hair and baby blues, had set her up with this guy!

What the actual fuck was up with that?

Little Gianni was a slob. Actually, he looked just like her Uncle Nico, and that was not a good thing. Seriously, not good at all.

He wore his hair slicked back in a too tight ponytail that emphasized his rapidly receding hairline. As if that wasn't enough to put her off, he was sporting an enormous paunch. Now, being a curvy girl, Elissa appreciated food and was in no way against men showing the same appreciation.

She liked bigger men. Always had. But bigger did

not mean you had to be sloppy. Little Gianni's stomach was literally hanging out from under a tight tan golf shirt that had definitely seen better days.

The man didn't even look like he had ever played a sport of any kind. With it, he wore brown polyester pants that were three inches above his ankles and unbuttoned at the waist.

He didn't look like he tried at all for this date. What kind of guy did that? His shirt collar was bent and wrinkled, and all three buttons were open to his chest, revealing a mat of oily, dark hair and pimples.

Somehow, he'd managed to tuck the back of the shirt in, but the front simply would not hold in that stomach. What worried her more were the tight brown pants.

As he sat back and stretched, she wondered if she should take cover. They looked like they were one bite from exploding off his body. Elissa shuddered at the image.

Please God, if You have an ounce of mercy, don't let that happen, she prayed.

"Hang on, doll, I gotta take this," he said, and turned to answer his cell phone.

It was ringing to the tune of '70s disco music she hadn't heard since the last family reunion. Her eyes kept going to the huge stain on the front of his shirt. It was a little game she liked to call *what the hell is that*.

Coffee, she guessed.

"Up your ass, Bruno. I gotta have it by Monday," he cursed into the receiver.

Elissa winced at the spectacle he was making of them both. There were only a handful of people there, but still.

Deep breaths.

Ew. Maybe not.

She coughed as the strong body spray, that he'd obviously used a ton of in lieu of a shower, bad move in her opinion, invaded her lungs.

Oh, this was so bad.

Elissa was, by no means, a snob. But this guy looked like he'd stepped out of a bad 1980s mafia spoof film. What's worse, he kept smacking his lips together as he hung up the phone and looked her over from head to chest.

Thank fuck for the table, she thought, wishing she could hide her bosoms from his view.

"Ssssss," he hissed, like it was sexy or something.

She just grimaced. Elissa might be able to forgive a lot of quirks, but she hated mouth noises. Really hated them. It was a super pet peeve of hers. Never mind his totally inappropriate and unwelcomed leer.

She started counting the minutes, willing the date to be over already. Plenty of people would tell her she shouldn't be so choosy, but really? She was not this desperate.

Not yet anyway.

So, she was curvy and a little mouthy too. But was it wrong to want a man with good table manners? Even if men were thin on the ground for someone like her.

As a chef, she'd worked in a lot of restaurants and even as a personal cook for professional couples. She'd seen her fair share of unhappy couples and downright uncomfortable marriages. But as far as she was concerned, all relationships went downhill when good table manners were dismissed.

Good manners were merely a sign that a person was thoughtful and respectful. At least, that was what Nonna had told her. Gianni here had clearly missed that lesson as a child. Elissa had to work not to groan in disgust as he slurped a raw clam down his gullet.

Shudder.

Was there no end to his feeding? That's what it reminded her of. Feeding time at the zoo.

OMG. That was rude, she scolded herself. But it wasn't like she said it out loud.

All she wanted to do was go home. At least she was comfortable. *She'd* worn her softest pair of black leggings for this disaster date, paired with one of her favorite tunics on top.

It was dark green with tiny black buttons down the front and showed just the right amount of cleavage. She'd gone for neat and tidy as opposed to downright sexy.

Good call, in her opinion. Elissa looked perfectly fine for a nice *getting to know you* dinner, which is what she thought she was getting when her roommate asked her to step in for her on a blind date that one of her best client's had set up for her.

Elissa shuddered now, thinking how good old Gianni here would've reacted to the red dress and heels she'd contemplated before checking the weather report.

Gulp.

The lewd man was already salivating, and she was so not having it. Fending off his unwanted advances was not how she wanted to finish the night.

Ew again.

Elissa shivered, slightly chilled despite the fact they were indoors. It was a cold, gloomy evening, and the forecast called for even more rain later that night. Not at all unusual for this time of year in the Garden State.

November was always chilly in the evenings, rainy too. Elissa tended to run warm, but she was glad she'd brought a jacket with her. Especially since her date refused to turn the heat on in the car.

When she'd asked, he'd looked offended and told her it wasted gas.

Um. Okay.

She checked her phone. It was only seven o'clock, but the two hour drive was still ahead of them. Maybe they could make it home before ten if they left soon.

Ugh. Did he just blow his nose?

"Allergies, doll. Say, you gonna eat that?" he asked before scooping a fry from her dish and swallowing it down.

Elissa was gonna kill her roomie. Gretchen was a hair and nail stylist. A lot of her clients were elderly, and they just loved her. They were always offering to set her up on blind dates with their nephews and grandsons.

Mostly, the sweet old ladies were kind. They swore they could find her curvy roommate the right man, assuming she was single because she was new to town. Well, when Elissa got home tonight, she was going to tell Gretchen she needed to fire the old lady who set this date up from being her client.

Like *ASAP*.

No one who liked Gretchen would've sent her out with this guy. Gianni reached over and touched her hand and Elissa pulled back, reaching for the napkin.

Gross.

"I sure hope you ain't a cold one, doll," he said, shaking his head.

"What?"

"Ain't gonna matter. I know just what you need, doll."

She was still wiping the greasy residue he'd transferred to her skin from the food he ate sans utensils. This was too much. Elissa was beyond uncomfortable with all the leering and bad attempts at innuendo.

Plus, she was starving. One look at the dump he'd taken her to, and she knew she could never eat there. The chef in her wouldn't allow it.

To think they drove two hours for this! She'd practically frozen to death in his maroon Cadillac, listening to a CD of the Rat Pack, while Gianni crooned loudly, and off key, to the music.

Normally, she was a fan of the famous group of legendary singers. Having grown up in Hoboken, she couldn't not be a Sinatra fan. Though, to be honest, Dean Martin had always been her favorite.

Still, Elissa was a firm believer that there were just some people you did not try to imitate. Especially not if you were Little Gianni. While he was belting his heart out, he'd been trying to get his right hand on her thigh. She'd asked him politely to stop.

Twice.

Then she'd been forced to try something a little more drastic. Like spilling her hot tea on the offending hand the third time he'd tried it. Finally, he'd removed his hand from her leg. Not making a fourth attempt, which she was grateful for.

Elissa should've taken that behavior as a sign and gotten out of the car. But no. She'd wanted to do Gretchen a solid. So, against her better judgement, she gave the creep another chance.

Idiota, her grandmother's voice echoed in her brain again.

The old woman had loved her. Elissa knew that without a doubt. She'd raised her after her own parents had passed on in a tragic automobile accident when Elissa was just twelve.

Her grandmother was a no-nonsense kind of lady who dished out priceless wisdom with brutally honest insights. It was the same way she dished out huge bowls of pasta with her amazing meatballs and homemade sauce. Not to mention a side order of back-breaking hugs that Elissa still missed.

Nonna cooked like that all the time. She made a huge pot of sauce every weekend, and she was happy to serve it to Elissa and her teammates and friends, especially after games and tournaments.

Soccer had been her sport of choice, and cooking had soon become her favorite hobby. Her grandmother had encouraged her in both pursuits. Guiding her in one and cheering her on in the other. Elissa still missed her terribly.

"Hey babe, ain't you gonna eat nothin'? You know they charge twenty dollars just to sit down," Little Gianni interrupted her train of thought.

Elissa was forced to turn her mind back to the present, which unfortunately included watching, *and hearing*, him as he sucked on his teeth and stuffed another breaded shrimp down his throat.

"I'm fine," she answered with a polite smile plastered on her face.

Just get home, Lissa. Just get him to take you home.

Elissa closed her eyes when he looked back down at his dish. Thank God for small favors, she mused. At least he was more interested in eating at the moment.

He'd taken her to the rattiest looking hotel and casino she'd ever seen in her life. And the buffet room?

Ew.

Seriously, the place had to be violating at least a dozen health codes. When Gianni had said Atlantic City, she'd thought at least the atmosphere would be exciting. But they were so far from the real glitz and entertainment, they might as well be anywhere else.

She sighed, looking at the plate she'd made for herself. Elissa couldn't even fake an interest in the food. As a chef, it was hard enough to dine out.

She was always judging the food, the service, the ingredients. How could she not? It was her business. And that was when the food was good!

This was not good. Not at all.

She'd been to hospitals that served better food. Old yellow lights buzzed and blinked around the buffet, giving it an abandoned kind of feel. The menu was made up of mostly frozen then fried or baked cuisine.

Reheated actually. It was like a giant TV dinner buffet where every item was previously frozen when already cooked and warmed up in an oven.

It was the kind of food sold cheap at restaurant supply stores in bulk. Yeah, this was much worse than hospital food, in her opinion.

There was a worn carpet on the floor, a handful of scattered tables in the dining room, elevator music on in the background, and the entire place smelled like canned soup.

Not to mention not one of the five people there besides them was under sixty years old.

"Gianni," she said, leaning forward so as not to hurt his feelings.

"I thought you mentioned something about seeing a show tonight. Is it here?"

Please don't be here.

If he was taking her somewhere else, she could beg off and hire a cab to take her home. There was no way she was sitting through anything else with this man. Not now. Not ever.

"Ah, I see, babe, you want some entertainment first, I get it," he snickered loudly, and she blanched.

Whatever he thought was going to happen

wasn't. She needed to disabuse him of the notion, and fast.

"Alright, alright. Lemme finish this, babe. Then we'll go up to the room I got for us," he said.

Before she could make sense of the ludicrous statement, he slurped another fried shrimp, don't ask how. Then he grabbed her arm and yanked her from the seat before she could even react.

Elissa tugged on his hold, but the man was immovable. Tossing a five-dollar bill on the table, Little Gianni snatched a toothpick from the hostess stand before dragging her outside.

Great, he was a cheap tipper, too.

All she wanted was to go home. Figuring the best way to do that would probably be to get him to the car, she let him lead the way.

Once inside, she would ask him to drive back to Hoboken so she could wring Gretchen's neck. Fuming, she pulled her arm out of his hand and walked behind him.

The rain was really pouring, and the cheap bastard had refused valet. Elissa ducked her head so she wouldn't get so wet. Of course, the jacket she'd brought was light and had no hood.

Gianni had an umbrella, but he didn't offer to hold it for her, and honestly, she did not relish the idea of getting any closer to him than necessary.

Seriously, not happening.

Now all she had to do was break the news. She had no intention of watching a show or returning to the hotel with him.

What could go wrong?

Chapter Two

Uzzi Stregovich grunted happily as he opened the box of sweet-smelling, fresh pastries.

"I promise, *liebling*, I will only have one," he said aloud to his dearly departed wife.

Betty understood him well, and his love for sweets was no secret. Ah! How he missed the scrumptious little spiced cakes she used to bake for him on special occasions. Filled with currants and nuts, they were simply delicious. No one made them quite like her.

But it wasn't spiced cakes that had him salivating now. It was a box full of tasty treats from the flagship Bear Claw Bakery store in Barvale, New Jersey.

"Hank?" he called to his driver. "Are you sure you don't want?"

"No thank you, Uncle Uzzi. Better keep my eyes on the road," his driver replied.

Hank was one of his favorite honorary nephews, but the man did not know what he was missing.

Hmmm, Hank. No, no. That is for another time, Uzzi told himself.

His Magic buzzed around the small cab in the back of the limousine, but he was able to quiet it as he opened the thin cardboard box and peered inside. Sugary goodness wafted in the air, and Uzzi inhaled and sighed enthusiastically.

"It's been awhile, you know," he explained to no one in particular.

Hank was focused on the road, and no one else was there with him, but Uzzi peeked around before snagging a delectable Bear Claw napoleon from the box.

"Oh! Perfection," he mumbled around a bite of custard filled, chocolate and vanilla glazed goodness.

The Bear Claw Bakery was one of the best in the entire country.

Hands down.

Once that one was gone, Uzzi grinned and dove for the fresh honey almond pastry, whose fragrance tantalized and tempted, even though he knew he should not have another. Not yet anyway. But how could he resist?

"I'm only human, *liebling*. Well, mostly," Uzzi said, conversing with his beloved Betty again.

He grinned, looking over the goodies and rubbed his hands together. What to try next? Such a big decision!

Wunderbar!

He thought and took another one from the box. This one dusted in powdered sugar and topped with a ripe strawberry slice.

Mmmm.

The pastries were just wonderful. There was nothing like the infamous Devlin brothers' sweets and Uzzi should know. He was a self-proclaimed pastry connoisseur.

The flagship store was a good hour out of the way from where he was headed, but worth it. So worth it.

They had the very best of what the brothers had to offer, in his opinion. Sometimes they were even made by one of the brothers themselves.

Like tonight. Lucky Uzzi.

That special little sixth sense he had told him that would be the case tonight. Magic had always been a friend to Uzzi Stregovich. When he asked Hank to make the detour, Uzzi hadn't been surprised to see the Alpha Black Bear of the Barvale Clan himself wiping his big hands on his apron before coming out to greet him.

He'd been friends with the Bear's father since back in the day. Marcus Devlin might have met his mate by chance on vacation, the Bear knew Uncle Uzzi's offer to consult with any members of the Clan was good for any time in the future. So long as Marcus promised to provide Uzzi with his decadent pastries whenever the old Witch was in town.

Like tonight.

Uzzi opened his cell phone while he took his first decadent bite of his third, or was it fourth, pastry? The famous black forest bear claw, he moaned and sighed. Cocoa powder and cherry filling had been added to the delicious morsel, making it a sinfully delicious way to end his gorging.

No more after this, liebling, I promise.

Just as he'd expected. The old Witch took another bite and reread the email he'd received earlier that week.

"Well Hank," he said aloud. "It seems the big bad pussy of Maverick Point has finally admitted he needs Uncle Uzzi's help to find a mate. Ha! What do you think about that?"

"Sounds like Hunter Maverick is making sense to me, boss," Hank replied.

Well, it wouldn't be the first time a pussy cat needed a Witch's help. Still, this was a special case. The *Neta*, or *Alpha* of the Maverick Tiger Pride, was having an issue with controlling his inner beast. That was never a good thing since Shifters, well, the whole supernatural world at large really, were kept secret from the humans, or *normals* as they were called by Magical beings.

This was not good. Rumors were spreading in Magical circles that Hunter's ability to control the Pride was waning. If whispered in the wrong ears, challenges would be issued. With challenges, came war, and how could anyone expect to keep a war secret in this technological age?

A problem, for sure! But Uzzi knew this was something that could be solved by finding the Neta his mate. A mated Tiger was a powerful, controlled Tiger. With something as precious as that to lose, no one would stand a chance against the naturally dominant male.

As it was, word had gotten around that the unmated Tiger was losing ground within his inner circle. Rumors were spreading that he was too weak to lead. Hunter's beast was on edge, and he was looking to Uncle Uzzi for help.

S hifters usually did at one time or other. A male Witch with a gift for matchmaking was rare for any age, but Uzzi had taken to his talents like a pro. He loved his work, and almost anyone would agree, it was a very interesting job. Besides, he could trace his roots back to the Goddess of Love herself.

Shifters operated a little differently than Witches, but not much has changed in the past hundred years far as Uzzi was concerned. It was troubling that so much talk was going on about the Neta of the Maverick Pride.

"Hank, correct me if I am wrong, but are open challenges still the preferred way for a Shifter to go after leadership of a Pack or pride?" he asked.

"Far as I know, yes," the driver replied.

"Hmm. Interesting. So if a Shifter has a leadership position, what is it based on?"

"Dominance for one," Hank explained. "Our animals can sense when a beast is more dominant. Challenges typically arise when two or more

Shifters in the same group exhibit the same level of dominance."

"And if the position was inherited?"

"It doesn't matter, Uncle Uzzi. You only keep power if you can beat everyone else. It seems pretty base, but there it is. Only the strongest earn the right to rule."

"I see," Uzzi replied.

It was all quite fascinating, and very different from how covens were run. Now, the way he saw it, the person, or persons, who started these rumors were not following typical protocol. That in itself was worrying.

Worse was the fact that since these whispers had started circulating, the Neta had been forced to ignore his business. Maverick Development was the largest demolition and construction firm in the area. It accounted for ninety percent of the Pride's income.

If forced to deal with the younger, and increasingly disrespectful, Pride members, to dispute these rumors, which Hunter had no choice but to do, then he was losing focus on the business. The firm needed to renew state and county contracts else take a pretty severe hit financially.

It was almost as if someone was gunning for the

man and the pride. Uzzi snorted. The entire situation was no good. Bad business all around, he thought, and wished he hadn't eaten all of that last pastry.

Of course, Uzzi wanted to help. Mount Maverick was a special community. A place Shifters were known as sort of an open secret. He didn't want anything bad to happen to the wonderful little town or the Maverick family.

That said, he'd asked Hank to drive him to South Jersey Pride to get a feel for the Neta's needs. By nature, Tigers were secretive, even in the Shifter world.

It was very telling that Hunter had come to a Witch with his problems at all. Serious business, indeed. Uzzi had dealt with his fair share of Tiger Shifters before, but he knew this situation would require something different.

Not that he was worried, of course. Uzzi trusted he could do the job as he had with countless other couples. The only thing that troubled him was the Tiger had not bothered talking about love, just mating.

Hmm.

That wouldn't work, but it was a detail Uncle Uzzi was sure he could iron out with the big guy. He already had a few prospects in mind for the striped pussy already, but he was still contemplating it.

"Excuse me, Uncle Uzzi?" Hank looked at him through the rearview mirror.

Uzzi never bothered to raise the partition between them, but he jumped all the same. Sometimes, when he was deep in thought, Uzzi was easily startled. A clap of thunder sounded overhead, and he gasped again.

"You okay, sir?"

"Yes, Hank, don't mind me. It happens with increased age," he replied grimly.

"Oh, well, um---"

"Yes, Hank? Spit it out, man," Uzzi wiped his mouth on a napkin and met the man's eyes.

"Well, I think I see someone walking on the side of the road," Hank said, slowing the car and leaning closer to the glass of the windshield.

"In this weather?" Uzzi asked, mouth open as lightning flashed in the sky.

"Yes," Hank said, slowing down even more.

"It appears to be a woman. She has no umbrella, either."

Uzzi paused for a moment. His Magic was alert and zipping all around him excitedly. Whoever this damsel was, she needed his help. Uzzi had never failed to offer aid to a lady, and he sure as heck would not start now.

Is this your work, liebling?

A small smile teased the corner of his mouth. Uzzi's beloved wife, Betty, had always been able to spot a mate faster than old Uzzi ever could.

"Well, let's stop this thing, and see if the lady needs a ride before she drowns out there!"

Uzzi inched towards the window and peeked out, using his Magically enhanced vision to catch sight of the female his driver had spied.

Yes, she was a woman, alright. Soaking wet, but nicely shaped. He did not mind pointing out the obvious physical attractions of the female, with all due respect, of course.

Uzzi was a widower, a Witch, but ultimately, a matchmaker. Looks were important, not as much as what was on the inside, but important still, at least to his clients. Shifters especially had physical demands that were not for the faint of heart, or hip, he thought with a mischievous chuckle.

Ah! What could be better than this? Helping others find love, to celebrate life, and to live in peaceful harmony until the end of days.

So yes, he looked her over with the discerning eye of a matchmaker. The female was curvy and cute, just the way Shifters preferred their women. As the car inched over to the side of the road, Uzzi lowered his window and put on his most friendly smile.

Big brown eyes blinked down at him, rapidly against the fat drops of rain that seemed determined to get in her way.

"Hello there, young lady, it looks like you could use a lift," Uzzi said kindly.

Chapter Three

It was in his favor that Uzzi was older now. He had thick white hair and a beard to match, light blue eyes, and a ready smile for all and any. A good Witch, he'd used his Magic throughout the years to spread joy and happiness. His matchmaking efforts had been praised far and wide, and he truly enjoyed the work.

Not an easy task. But when the Goddess of Love herself was a descendant, it wasn't as if he'd had much choice. Uzzi Stregovich was one of the lucky ones. He'd found happiness in his calling.

"Well, how do I know you're not a serial killer?" the female asked.

That made Uzzi grin. The girl had spunk.

Nice. Very nice.

"Listen to me now, young lady, I swear on my beloved wife's grave, killing you is the last thing on my mind. Take a leap of faith and get in. You might not be so lucky with the next car that stops," he added.

The woman looked at Uzzi, then at his driver. She was still mulling it over when suddenly, a deafening roar of thunder sounded overhead, and lightning struck a tree not twenty feet away from them. That got her moving.

"Okay, I'll get in, but if you decide to kill me, give me some warning first, okay?"

"Sure, I promise," Uzzi flashed a warm smile and opened the door.

He liked this girl. She had plenty of sass. Not to mention plenty of curves that his Shifter clients were incredibly fond of. He wondered if she liked cats. Big ones.

Hmm.

The wheels in his head started working overtime, and with it, his Magic began to hum and vibrate. Ah, yes, this one was special. But before he got into all of that, Uzzi would have to do something about this shivering little creature.

"Here, take this and try to warm up," Uncle Uzzi said.

He handed the stranger a small travel blanket that had been tucked in one of the limo's many compartments. Once she wrapped it around her, Uzzi turned the heat on high.

"There, that should help."

"Thank you. I am so sorry to get your car all wet," the stranger said through her chattering teeth.

"Don't give it another thought, dear. Now, my name is Uzzi Stregovich. I am a widower, and this is Hank, my driver."

"Miss," Hank said, nodding as he pulled carefully back out onto the road.

"I'm Elissa Phoenix, but my friends call me Lissa."

"How did you get stranded here at this time of night, Lissa?" Uzzi asked.

"It's a long story," she sighed, and shivered slightly.

"How about some tea or coffee to warm you up? There is water in the little machine just there. Pick out your own tea or coffee pod and press the button on top," he instructed.

Uncle Uzzi nodded as Elissa looked over the offerings. She chose a peppermint tea pod and popped it into the amazing little gadget. Almost as wondrous as Magic, the old Witch mused.

He waited as she filled the insulated travel mug

and added a touch of honey. Elissa leaned forward and allowed the steam from the mug to warm her chilled face before returning her gaze to his.

"I love peppermint tea. Thank you so much," she smiled and blew on her tea from the small opening on top of the mug.

Always a good idea before sipping any hot liquid. Uzzi approved of her methodical and careful maneuvering.

"Better now?"

"Yes, much. If you could just take me to the nearest town, I am sure I could find some public transportation to get back home."

"Where is home? If you don't mind me asking," Uzzi said casually.

"Hoboken for now."

"Hoboken? My, that is a way away! Excellent Italian bread bakeries there. In particular, Marie's and Dom's."

"My grandmother loved them! Anyway, I know it is far. Uh, it's kind of a long story," Elissa said, shaking her head.

"Now, you might as well tell me what happened, unless you have something better to do?" Uncle Uzzi teased.

"I'm sorry, of course. You see, I was on a blind

date with this guy, and well, it went bad. The guy was just a real creep," she shook her head.

"I see. He didn't hurt you, did he?" Uzzi asked, sitting up straight.

He noticed Hank listening too, and the man's eyes flashed with anger. One thing Uzzi could not tolerate was any kind of abuse aimed at a female. His own blue eyes were undoubtedly glowing with his Magic. The powers within him were zapping around in a frenzy at the idea of any woman being hurt by a man.

"No," she replied, quieting both Uzzi's Magic and Hank's beast with the simple truth.

"He was just expecting a different kind of outcome for this evening and when I asked to be taken home, he wanted what I considered an unfair exchange. So, I slapped his face and walked out on him," she shrugged.

"That was very brave of you."

"Well, my grandmother didn't raise me to be bullied into doing anything I didn't want to do. And Little Gianni was definitely something I did not want to do."

"That bad, huh?"

"Worse. I swear, I am going to kill my roommate when I get back home. And judging by the email I just got from our realtor, it looks like it will only be home for a little while longer. They are hiking up our rent again."

"Oh my! But why kill your roommate?" Uzzi asked only half joking.

He liked this girl and had a feeling he'd met her on the road for a special reason.

"Well, for one thing, it was her date. I only took her place to be nice. As for the other, living in Hoboken is so expensive and with this new increase, I don't know if Gretchen and I can afford to live there anymore," Elissa sighed and shook her head.

"I see. Tell me, Elissa, what do you do for a living?"

Elissa looked up, and her brown eyes warmed for a second. Uzzi watched her think it over before she spoke, another good sign. Then she smiled, and he was sold.

She likes her work. She needs sanctuary. She has much to offer. This is good. Very good.

"I'm a personal chef. I go to people's houses and cook and prepare them meals for the day or week, however many times a week they need. Of course, my best clients recently moved, so I am always looking for more work. Things are rough right now," she said.

"Didn't enjoy working in restaurants?" Uzzi asked.

"Not really. Too many people. I like to be one on one with my clients. To see to their personal needs. Some have dietary restrictions and I have to work with that. It is very rewarding, actually."

"Like taking care of a family?" Uzzi asked.

"Yes," Elissa replied.

He thought he saw a glint of something wistful in her eyes. Like she was seeing a memory she seldom looked at anymore flitter through her brain.

"I grew up with just my grandma, but we were a family. Kids from my soccer team always showed up on Sundays to eat with us because we made so much food. I love cooking for people. There is just something great about it. I hope to have a family someday to cook for, but it's not likely." Elissa sighed.

"I may know of a place that is looking for a personal chef. Not a restaurant, more of a family type situation. But I warn you they have big appetites," Uzzi hedged.

He was not lying. The Maverick Pride Neta did ask for someone who could cook. A female who would not balk at the idea of working with and for her Pride. Someone who was nurturing, caring, who would want cubs.

Hmm.

Elissa was at a crossroads. Something had to give, and soon. She seemed honest, hardworking, and she was positively lovely, in Uncle Uzzi's opinion.

He believed in Fate, that was a must in his line of work, and so, Uzzi wondered if these two souls might not be just right for each other. Perhaps he'd know with a few more details.

"A job for me? Really? That's awesome. Where did you say it was?"

"That is the thing, my dear. It is more a live-in position."

"I would have to live there?"

"Yes, but I am more betting you would want to live there. If you would like to see it, I happen to be on my way there now. You could come with me and interview for the job tonight."

"But I'm a mess-"

"Oh, don't worry, my dear. You will be fine once you dry up a bit, and you can always freshen up there."

Elissa bit her lip. She was worried. Not good. Uzzi needed to put her at ease.

"I would never take you someplace that isn't safe, Elissa. Mount Maverick is just over in Burlington county. It's a small community, and the leader there is a good man."

"You mean like the mayor?" She asked.

"Something like that, Elissa," Uzzi began. and leaned forward, trusting his instincts not for the first time in his very long life.

"I know tonight was bad for you, Elissa Phoenix, and you don't know me very well, but may I ask you something?"

"Um, yeah, I guess."

"What kind of man are you looking to settle down with?"

"What? Oh. Um, I don't know." Elissa laughed and pointed to herself.

"I mean, I'm not exactly overcome with offers."

"Nonsense! You are just beautiful, young lady. A rival for my Betty, here take a look at this," Uzzi said and reached inside his wallet for the snapshot he always carried of his *liebling*.

"Awww, she's beautiful," Elissa replied.

"Now, if you could pick any attributes in a man, what would they be?"

"Okay. Top of my head, if I was searching for a boyfriend, I guess I would want someone who was honest, loyal, and kind. Someone who is attracted to me, you know," she said and blushed sweetly,

"Someone who loves me and wants me for who I am."

"I see. Very levelheaded. And what about looks?"

"I don't think I should be too picky about that," she shrugged.

"Now explain to me why a young girl like you can't have any man she wants? Come on, it's just us, Elissa. What kind of man is a young beauty like you attracted to?"

"That's an odd question for a man, no?"

"It might seem that way, but it is an industry thing, I assure you. Here," he reached into his pocked, and retrieved a business card, handing it to the no longer shivering female.

"You just think of me as Uncle Uzzi. I run this service here. now, you would be doing me a favor if you answered my questions. What else is there to do? Besides, I so love a good chat."

"Alright, but only because you asked," Elissa said and snuck a peek at Hank and leaned forward to whisper.

"I love guys with muscles who are *bigger* than me. Not that I know many muscly guys who like chubby girls, but I swear, there is just something about a big man that makes me feel small and safe."

"And sex? You do enjoy a healthy sexual appetite in a man, yes?" Uzzi asked.

"Um, that's a little personal, Uncle Uzzi---"

"My wife, gods rest her, loved intimacy above all else. She always said that couples or mates came together this way to express what words could not. To reaffirm vows and show their love for one another. Sex is natural, Elissa. It is important too. We are physical beings who walk this earth, do you not agree? I swear I miss that as much as I miss her cooking," he said truthfully.

"Oh! Well, I never thought about it that way. I mean, I guess I must seem prudish, but honestly, my sex life is a bit of a disaster. In fact, I haven't had any great sex that I know of, but yes, I agree with your wife. I suppose physical intimacy is important," Elissa said in a rush.

She blushed furiously, but Uzzi Stregovich was on a roll. He nodded sagely, reading between the lines. After all, he would be negligent if he did not ask such intimate questions. Prospective mates needed to know the deal.

When matchmaking Shifters, blunt talk was required. Once she noted Uzzi's interest was not personal, Elissa had no problem opening up to him as he knew she would.

"Oh dear, you will know great sex when you have it. In my experience, the best sex only happens where there is love," Uzzi winked.

"There is nothing as fulfilling as making love to someone you were made to be with. Destiny, you know."

"Destiny? Well, great. Then since I am thinking up this dream guy, sure, great sex is a must."

"Good, I think I know just the man for you."

Elissa laughed, and Uzzi just smiled at her. It was so sad, he thought, how many women settled for a mediocre sex life. Life was short, why not spend it with someone who could give you tantalizing days and sizzling nights?

"How can you do that?" Elissa asked.

"Read the card, dear," he said, and she looked down.

"Uncle Uzzi's Magical Matchmaking Service---"

"Yes! That is me," he replied jovially.

"Oh, no thanks. I told you about my date tonight. I am just not interested in any more blind dates."

"I understand but give me a moment to explain to you about my agency and I promise, you will see it's not like the others."

"Yeah," she scoffed. "Magical, right?"

"Yes. It is Elissa. Just like me," Uzzi replied and held out his palms.

In the center of his outstretched hand, dozens of Magical sparkles zipped and zoomed, twirling round and round until they created a glittery, dime-sized zephyr. Elissa gasped.

"OHMYGAWD! What is that? What are you?"

"Think of me as your fairy godfather, Elissa. Only, I am not a fairy, you see, I am a Witch."

"I thought Witches were old hags who rode brooms."

"My Aunt Helga, for sure, but no, my dear, I too am a Witch. Males and females born with Magic are both called Witches. Now, enough about me. Have you ever heard of Shifters?"

"Wow, I did not know that! Wait? Shifters? Like the kind in those paranormal romance novels told by writers like P. Mattern, Julia Mills, and Gina Kincade?" Elissa asked and quirked her head.

"Exactly! What if I tell you they are real?"

"I don't know. *Are* you telling me they are real?"

Elissa sat straight, her intense brown eyes seriously considering the possibility. Uzzi chuckled. Yes. This woman was perfect for what he had in mind.

"Yes, I am," Uzzi replied. "Shifters, Witches, and more than you can imagine are out there, living and breathing, sharing this world with humans like you. The real question, Elissa, is do you think you are ready to live in that world?"

Uzzi allowed some of his Magic out. The sparks pulsed with warmth and circled the pair of them. Power would be glowing in his eyes right about then, and he waited until Elissa registered that she was seeing something very real, and very different from her norm.

Elissa was witnessing his powers, and he, in turn, was introducing her to the supernatural world. A punishable crime for his kind, but it was a chance he was willing to take.

"Wow," she whispered, reaching out to touch a spark.

"I don't know what to say."

"Well, the fact you aren't screaming tells me you might be just what I am looking for," Uzzi sat back in the cushioned leather seats and began to explain a little bit about the matchmaking service and what he did for a living.

"So, you find people their mates? That's like a husband or wife?" Elissa asked, catching on right away.

"Yes, I do. Now, how would you like your own muscle bound Shifter who would worship and love you no matter what? Not to mention pleasure you sexually in ways you can't even imagine," he smiled again, liking Elissa's reaction.

The young woman's eyes bulged, and she swallowed hard.

"Are you serious?"

"As a heart attack."

"Mr. Stregovich, *er*, Uncle Uzzi," she said, when he mock frowned.

"If you could find me a match like that, I wouldn't kick him out of my bed. Seriously though, I would certainly be indebted to you. But do you think you can find someone for me? I mean, what Shifter would want *me* as a mate?"

"Oh Elissa, you make me smile, you do. And I am happy to do this thing for you. Look, I promise you I can find a mate for you. It is what I do."

"Okay, then. I am game."

"Excellent. You won't be sorry. All of my couples wind up *purrfectly mated*."

Chapter Four

Elissa blinked at the elfish man sitting across from her. She looked down at the business card she still held in her hand.

Uncle Uzzi's Magical Matchmaking Service.

Disbelief warred with hope inside her chest. All her life, she loved myths, legends, fairytales, and folklore. She'd waited and hoped and dreamed with all her heart, wanting to believe her prince was out there somewhere searching for her.

Fuck being politically correct.

Elissa Phoenix was a dreamer. Always had been. She might be short, curvy and she damn well could out cuss a sailor, but dammit, she was worthy of love.

Was it wrong of her to want someone who made

her feel feminine and cherished? Someone who wanted her body, heart, soul, and mind. A man who cared about her happiness and was thoughtful enough to ask after her feelings at the end of the day.

Maybe dreams really can come true, Elissa thought, staring at the cheerful older man.

She didn't normally go with her gut, but something about Uncle Uzzi simply radiated honesty, charm, and trustworthiness. If he was a Witch, like he said, then he was a good one. She felt no ill will or bad vibes from the white bearded fellow.

Maybe tonight was a turning point for her. It sure as hell beat most of the nights she'd endured the past few years.

True, Little Gianni had ditched her on the side of the road when she refused to play footsies with the smelly creep. Almost immediately after jumping out of his car, rain had started pouring down from the skies in buckets.

Thunder had roared, and lightning struck overhead, making her heart race and her pulse speed. Elissa had been cold, wet, angry, and terrified all at the same time.

But then, just as suddenly, her luck had changed. Uzzi Stregovich and his straight-faced driver had found her on the side of the road. He'd offered a friendly smile, shelter from the rain, and a blanket to dry herself.

The stretched limo was warm and toasty, the peppermint tea perfectly hit the spot. Elissa looked at the grandfatherly man who'd just claimed Shifters actually existed and thought about her options.

So, not only were fairy tale creatures real, but Uzzi Stregovich ran some sort of matchmaking service for them. Elissa had been on bad dates, but she'd never considered a service before. Maybe it was time.

"*Uncle Uzzi's Magical Matchmaking Service,*" she said aloud.

"That's right," he agreed, his slight accent making her grin.

Elissa could not have made this up if she'd tried. Magic was real. Holy fuck! She'd felt the little shocks of electricity racing up her arm when the elderly man had handed the rectangular bit of better than average card stock to her.

Maybe it was the fact she was still wet from the rain. But she knew better than to try to make sense of it.

Magic was real, she thought again.

Anyone else and Elissa might have thought they were crazy or high on something illegal. But not him. Uncle Uzzi was simply too honest, too amiable, and too darn adorable. He really was like a tiny Santa, or a fairy godfather like he'd said!

So, she thought, *Shifters. Yeah. Reality. Gulp.*

Elissa had always been a woman of faith, and something was telling her to trust her instincts. An avid reader, she cut her teeth on romance novels growing up. Sure, she loved the big wigs like Steele and Roberts, but it was the indies who held her heart.

Her absolute, most secret, favorite stash of books included stories about Werewolves and other Shifter heroes who found their happily-ever-afters with regular, and often curvy, women. Women who looked just like Elissa.

Society's representation of women had somewhat changed in the past decade, but curvy was often accompanied by hurtful and judgy comments that she was unhealthy or would look better after losing a few pounds. The world was crazy for thin people. And she just wasn't thin.

She was a chef, so she knew healthy food. Her cooking was full of fresh veggies, lean meats, and whole grains. It didn't matter. Her body just loved her chub.

Maybe Uncle Uzzi could help her find a man who would love it as well...

Life was too short for her to not love herself. Why shouldn't she have a piece of pie, *or a bear claw*, once in a while? Elissa worked hard, and she appreciate good food. Nothing wrong with that in her book.

"Thanks," she said, taking the proffered treat.

"You know, you are taking this all with an even keel," Uncle Uzzi spoke up, interrupting her reverie.

"I know," Elissa smiled around a mouthful of the best bear claw she had ever eaten.

Who knew they made these things with cocoa powder in the crust? That wasn't all, the pastry had the best cherry filling she had ever tasted. It was her favorite flavor. She made a mental note to get the address of the baker who made the amazing pastry from Uncle Uzzi. It wasn't often she was impressed by someone else's cooking, but this was phenomenal.

"I guess I've always wondered about stuff like that. You know, the *unknown*. Anyway, I like to read in between cooking jobs," she replied and shrugged.

"I see," Uzzi said, offering her a napkin.

She felt her cheeks heat as she took one and wiped some cherry filling from her lips.

"It just makes sense to me that there is more in this world than we could ever know."

"Well, I'm glad you feel that way. We should be there any minute," Uncle Uzzi smiled.

"Who are we meeting and where exactly?"

"Maverick Point is in Burlington County. It is a mostly Shifter town with some normals. Mount Maverick looms beautifully in the background and there is a lovely creek that cuts through it. In the winter, it looks like something out of a Rockwell painting."

"Sounds amazing, But how is it mostly Shifters live there? Don't regular people find out?"

"Well, the secret is safe since nearly everyone who lives there is either mated to a Shifter or has one somewhere in the family tree."

"I had no idea something like that could even happen."

"It is a small town. We're headed to see the Neta, that's another word for Alpha or leader of the Pride. His name is Hunter Maverick."

"Maverick? I see, so he's like the big man about town," she said, feeling her stomach clench at the mere mention of the man's name.

"Hunter is a good man. He is the man I was hired

to help with my special services, and the man I want you to meet."

"Really? But I thought I was here for a job?" She swallowed again.

"You are, but hopefully you will find more than a job here. Elissa Phoenix, I believe you will find your destiny."

Elissa sat there and let his words sink in. Her destiny? Holy cow.

"Now, listen to me, if you feel uncomfortable in any way, you say the word, and we will leave. You are under no obligation to stay there. Do you understand?"

"Yes, I understand. But why would you do that for me?" she said.

"Elissa, I might work for the Neta, but my first duty is to keep you safe. Besides, we are friends now, aren't we?"

"I think we are," Elissa replied after a moment of consideration.

"Uncle Uzzi?"

"What is it dear?"

"You said he's a Tiger Shifter? Like, as in a real *tiger*?"

"Shifters can be much larger than their wild cousins, Elissa. He is probably twice the size of a normal tiger when he is in his fur, but don't worry, trust your destiny. Hunter Maverick will not harm you. He couldn't."

"I don't understand."

"When a Shifter finds his mate, his entire world revolves around her. Keeping her with him safe, happy, protected, and satisfied sexually, of course, is all his beast will tolerate. His mate becomes his primary focus," Uzzi winked, and Elissa felt herself blush.

It all sounded good to her. But what were the odds some sexy as sin Pride leader was going to want a very curvy, potty mouth, curly blonde-haired Italian girl with no family, from Hoboken, New Jersey as his mate?

She swallowed hard as the limo slowed down in front of one of the largest homes she'd ever seen. New Jersey had more than its share of uncommonly large estates, but this was stunning.

It was a sprawling three story manse with a huge, two-level wraparound porch and floor to ceiling windows on every floor. The whole thing seemed to be made of glass and wood and stone. It was structurally amazing, and so very unique, she hardly knew where to look. Even with the rain falling, it was beautiful.

Huge oaks and beeches lined the front of the enormous lawn, and she was pleased to see a full dozen dwarf maples as well. Their leaves were a mix of bright red to deep purple, all beautiful and lush, proclaiming Fall in the Garden State like nothing else could.

Oh shit.

Was that a tiger lying across what looked like an extra wide gliding bench up on the porch? The enormous beast was staring lazily at the rain from his perch.

Why shouldn't he, she thought wryly. He was dry and comfy, content to just stay where he was. He was huge, with thick red fur lined with black stripes and a lighter underbelly. Elissa had seen tigers during trips to the zoo, but nothing like this.

"Oh my," Elissa whispered.

She noted the gorgeous beast lazing about under the protective cover of the porch, watching them with a steady gaze that belied his demeanor. The creature was taking them in carefully, weighing the threat even as the storm began to build. Rain and lightning lashed out all around them.

"What are you looking at, dear?" Uncle Uzzi asked as Hank came around with an umbrella to help them out of the car.

"That sure is a pretty boy," Elissa said, nodding towards the beast.

"Yes, most pussies are," Uncle Uzzi agreed with a sly grin.

She giggled and tsked at the older man. He was so bad! And completely endearing, like a sweet, funny, and extra sassy godfather. Uncle Uzzi wiggled his nose and a few blue sparks seemed to appear out of nowhere, zapping the big cat on the butt.

Elissa choked on the piece of gum she'd been chewing, and he patted her gently on the back.

"Uncle Uzzi, I think you're more troublemaker than matchmaker, for sure!"

"My dear Betty thought so," he agreed, and laughed aloud.

"I think I'd like to be you when I grow up," Elissa said, smiling as she took his proffered arm.

"Oh no, my dear, a beard would not look right on that pretty face," Uncle Uzzi teased.

Uzzi winked at Elissa, and together they walked in step with Hank as he held the large umbrella overhead, shielding them as they walked towards the front door. Moving past the large wild cat without so much as a blink, Uncle Uzzi ushered Elissa into the unlocked entryway and through a large anteroom.

"Wow," Elissa gasped as she took in the enormous open floor plan of the space.

"This place is gigantic."

"Yes, well, it needs to be, you see, this is the Pride House. A meeting place of sorts, for the entire Maverick Pride. The Neta lives here with some of his closest Pride members, though I assume he has his own section," Uncle Uzzi explained as they walked down the hall and into a very large living room.

"Have you been here before?"

"Not in a very long time," Uncle Uzzi said and looked around the almost empty room.

A huge man with short reddish-brown hair sprung up from the couch and walked towards them with his brows furrowed.

"You can't just walk in here," the stranger began.

"Hello, Blake," Uncle Uzzi said, one eyebrow raised at the man's snarky tone.

"It is Blake, isn't it? Pride Beta and Tiger Shifter originally from Washington, D.C.?"

"How do you know that?" he asked.

The stranger's mud brown eyes went wide with shock and annoyance. He barely gave her a passing glance, but he was rude and snarly as he squared off against sweet Uncle Uzzi.

Elissa hoped this wasn't the man Uzzi had in mind. She already didn't think much of his attitude or bad manners.

"You met Hunter at college as I understand it, but you have no other connections, no family or old Pride, yes?" Uncle Uzzi continued, unbothered by the growling.

He spoke as if completely unaffected by the massive man, whereas Elissa wanted to hide behind something. The stranger's entire vibe was hostile and unwelcoming.

"I don't know who the hell you two think you are spouting whatever mumbo jumbo you feel like, but you can't just walk in here like you own the place!"

Hank moved forward, but Uncle Uzzi raised one wrinkled hand to stop him. In awe of the small, elderly man's courage, Elissa remained still.

"Who I am, is Uzzi Stregovich. Now listen, you unlicked cub, go tell Hunter Maverick I am here." Uncle Uzzi's firm voice brooked no interruption.

Elissa decided then and there to take a page from Uncle Uzzi's book. She stood her ground next to the shorter man, remaining still as the stranger's golden gaze landed right on her. She might not be a Shifter, but that didn't mean she was a pushover.

Hell no.

Chapter Five

Blake looked from Uzzi to Elissa, his lip curled in a threatening snarl. His posture was stiff, and he looked ready to pounce.

Elissa narrowed her gaze, eying the rude sonovabitch right back as he insolently looked her over. She cringed internally as he took his time, raking his cold brown eyes over her wide hips and ample breasts.

Stopping to stare pointedly where she did not want him looking, Blake smirked and this time she was the one who felt like growling. He was totally creeping her out.

If this was what Shifters were like, maybe she made a mistake coming here with Uncle Uzzi. The old Witch was kind and honest, but this guy was a fucking jerk. She knew jerks. Had dated them in the past.

"Did you not hear me?" Uzzi repeated, and Elissa saw sparks zipping along his fingertips.

"Uzzi, maybe we should just---"

"Listen to the human, old man," Blake said in a deep, guttural voice.

What the heck? Elissa narrowed her eyes at him. She certainly didn't want to tuck tail and run. Not now anyway.

"I will leave by order of the Neta, and no one else," Uzzi stated calmly.

You sure about that, old man?"

Elissa ground her teeth together, not liking the glint of hostility in Blake's suddenly orange gaze. She moved slightly in front of Uzzi. Without really understanding why or where she got the courage, Elissa opened her mouth to tell Blake to back the fuck up when another stranger walked into the room.

A resounding growl emanated from the man, though she didn't see his mouth open. It was coming up from his chest, vibrating through his whole body, and making everyone stand at attention. She glanced at Uzzi, but the elderly Witch merely bowed his head politely, then he straightened and positively beamed at the guy.

"Ah, there you are!"

Oh shit.

Was this the guy Uncle Uzzi had been telling her about? The male was enormous, larger than the first jack-hole they'd met. Taller by only a few inches, but nearly half again as wide.

His head was closely shaved, leaving Elissa to wonder the color and texture. Was it brown or blond? Straight or wavy.? Odd to have such thoughts at a time like this, but all she wanted to do was get closer to him. To put her hand on that massive rumbling chest and soothe whatever had angered him.

Blake had her hackles up, but this guy made her want to turn belly up and pant like a puppy, begging for attention. She shook her head, as if to break the seductive spell that had come over her with his entrance. But there was simply no denying it.

She wanted him, and that was insane. Elissa was hardly promiscuous, and she'd never wanted to bang a guy on sight. But from the moment she spotted him, it was as if a wave of lust had washed over her. There was more to it than that, she acknowledged as she tried to categorize her feelings.

His mere presence was soothing, calming the nerves Blake had frazzled so relentlessly. She felt safe, curious, and very drawn to him even, despite the strange situation.

Hunter Maverick, leader of the Pride, was gorgeous. He had a healthy tan despite the season, leaving her to believe he worked outdoors. Maybe alongside his construction crew, she mused.

Something about a man who worked with his hands really turned her on. His dark eyebrows framed his face in a natural arch over the most electrifying, teal-colored eyes she had ever seen.

That laser like gaze of his flashed to her before going back to the other man, the one she did not like. He seemed pissed.

Oh yes, please.

Elissa had never been a fan of men with overly dominant personalities, and this guy was that. And so much more, she thought, even as heat filled her veins.

He moved silently, confidently, taking up the space between her and the hostile stranger. The guy oozed power. One hundred percent alpha male. A Shifter, definitely, and she wondered how she'd never noticed them before. If they were all like this, people were bound to figure it out.

Besides, a normal human would overdose on the amount of testosterone this guy had in his system. Judging from the look on the other guy's face, the creep knew it as well.

"Move," the newcomer said in a voice so deep and growly it did funny things to her insides.

That's all he said.

One word.

Move.

He had the air of a man who expected to be obeyed. This gorgeous stranger had simply slid into the miniscule space between her and Blake, so close she could feel the heat radiating off him in tempting waves as if he were her own personal furnace. Like he had every right to occupy that space, *her space* if she were being a brat about it.

And there he stood, facing down the enemy, like he was her own brand spanking new self-appointed protector.

Yes, please.

Surprisingly, Elissa was totally okay with it. Sure, she believed in feminism, but there was no way in hell she was getting between two grown ass men who came with their own sets of claws and fangs.

Not today.

Odd that she should feel so drawn to the man.

She didn't know him from Adam, and like she mentioned before, Elissa hated alpha-holes. On the contrary, her body really seemed into them. In fact, his macho display had a very curious effect on her. *Especially her panties.*

Thank goodness she was already wet from the rain, or someone might notice. She squirmed slightly, and the man went still. His back was to her, but she swore he closed his eyes and breathed in deep, swaying slightly on his very sturdy looking feet. His very presence made the other man shrink before her eyes.

Move.

The word still reverberated in the air. The command unmistakable. Blake did move. Immediately, in fact. If he was his animal right then, she'd imagined he'd have tucked his tail between his legs. He'd probably run too. Far, far away from the big bad stranger. The image caused her to snort, and she covered her mouth, horrified to have made such a sound.

The man turned to face her, amusement clear on his handsome mien. Intense teal eyes bore into hers as he turned his full attention, and, as a result, all that powerful animal magnetism on Elissa. She licked her lips and stared back.

"Who are you?"

His deep voice held an edge she didn't recognize, but she liked it. He growled the words more than said them, moving in on her like a predator did his prey. Her stomach tensed and a slow, deep ache began to build inside her.

Holy shit!

Her nipples hardened beneath her damp shirt and bra, and her pussy positively throbbed at the intensity of his stare. She was completely aware of him as a man, and it was the first time in her life she'd ever felt anything so damn hot.

Yes, he exuded authority, but he didn't frighten her. On the contrary, she was turned on by all that masculinity and his innate sex appeal. He leaned in close, too close. Really, she should've moved away, but she was rooted to the spot.

Was he going to kiss her? But no, the stranger turned his head, pressing his nose almost against her as he sniffed the air at the base of her neck. He let out a sort of chuffing noise, his hot breath tickling her exposed skin. Elissa nearly creamed her panties.

His low growl grew louder. She could practically feel the vibrations through her own body. Somehow, he moved in even closer, so close they were a hair away from touching.

Frozen like a deer in headlights, she was aware of her inability to move. But she couldn't help it. Elissa was powerless to do anything but breathe while his eyes glittered at her. She felt hunted, not in a bad way exactly, but still. Finally, she backed up a step.

Uh oh.

She almost screamed when he followed. Apparently, retreating was a miscalculation on her part. Predators liked to chase. He was definitely a predator. And that would make her the prey.

Gulp.

"Your name?" he asked again.

The big man lifted an impossibly large hand and held a damp lock of hair off her shoulder, pressing it to his nose. He moaned as he sniffed her golden curls, eyes questioning as he hit her with their full intensity once more.

"Why are you wet?"

"Uh, it's raining," was her immediate response.

"Name?"

"I'm, uh, my name is-"

A shake of a familiar white head behind him reminded her she was not alone with the mountain of a man.

Sad sigh.

"Back off, Hunter. Give the lady room to breathe," Uncle Uzzi said, clearly exasperated.

A rounded, and short, body gently pushed its way between them, and Elissa found herself staring at the back of Uncle Uzzi's thick white hair. He dug a stick of some sort into the man's chest and shoved him back an inch.

"Hunter, really, you exasperate me," he said, but the Tiger still didn't move.

"Bad kitty! We do not paw at ladies!"

"Uzzi? You brought her?" The man asked, seemingly stunned.

"Now, I thought from the tone of your letter you needed this situation resolved as soon as possible, so I headed out to see you almost immediately. I was in the area, anyway."

"I see," he said, clearing his throat and moving back an inch.

Was it wrong Elissa wanted to shove Uzzi out of the way to get closer to the stranger?

Probably.

Okay, fine. Definitely wrong.

Bad girl!

"I apologize for my behavior, Mr. Stregovich. My Tiger is pushing harder than ever, but good news. I believe you have brought me the *purrfect* solution to soothe my beast," he said, speaking in a low voice.

Elissa still made out the slight tip of his head in her direction from where she was standing behind Uncle Uzzi. The acknowledgement made her giddy to her utmost mortification.

"I can see that. Give us a second, please. Hunter! Shoo," the older man said, and waved him away.

Hunter did move back. Barely. His eyes never leaving Elissa's face as he waited for them to converse in private.

"Uncle Uzzi, did you see that? He's so intense," she whispered and shivered.

It wasn't with fear. Not exactly. He was literally the biggest man she had ever seen. Hugely muscled with shoulders wider than a professional wrestler's. She felt drawn to him, mesmerized even, especially by those sexy as hell eyes.

Yes, he was a stranger. But he was really, *really* potent up close. And somehow, Elissa knew almost instinctively that he wouldn't harm her.

Her heart thudded in her chest, and she felt butterflies knocking around in her stomach. She wanted to walk around Uncle Uzzi, to put her arms around the man just to see for herself if he was a good fit. Though, honestly, somehow, she knew he would be.

A purrfect fit.

It was like something inside of her recognized him. Elissa felt light as air and a happy sort of anxiety washed over her. She wanted him. Like now.

Not to mention her knees were knocking from lusting after him so badly. Was this love at first sight? She didn't even know if she believed in such a thing, but no one else had ever made Elissa feel this way.

I should go.

Her mind agreed with the thought, but her heart screamed no. The silly organ wanted her to stay. To risk it all on the man with teal eyes who chuffed at her and stared so hard it made her panties wet.

"Look, dear," Uncle Uzzi interrupted her thoughts. "Think a moment, please. Shifters move fast, but if you need time, I will make sure you have it. In fact, if you say the word, we will leave right now. I know a Shifter's reaction can seem rather extreme if you're not used to them. I assure you, he will not hurt you, but you can move at your own pace. The decision is *yours* to stay or not."

Elissa knew what Uncle Uzzi meant, but her

heart skipped a beat, anyway. Besides, the Witch was wrong. Hunter Maverick could hurt her alright.

He could break my heart.

Elissa wasn't exactly fond of the possibility, but she knew she would regret it if she didn't at least see this thing through the beginning phase. People fell in love, or lust, at first sight all the time. Why should it be any different because those people turned into Tigers?

"I'll stay," she blurted, and the responding chuff coming from the big man made goosebumps pop out all over her.

"You're sure," Uncle Uzzi asked, his blue eyes peering into Elissa's.

"Yes. Will you introduce me? Please," she added.

Uncle Uzzi squinted at her for a moment. Magical sparks seemed to flit out from his being and circle her instantly, then he blinked, and they were gone. Uzzi squeezed Elissa's hand and nodded.

"Okay then, my dear."

Uncle Uzzi turned around and brought Elissa forward with a gentle hand on hers. He offered it to Hunter, who touched her fingertips so lightly she hardly felt him at all. The big man was trembling from head to toe, and Elissa felt as if she were in a trance.

Something was happening right then. Something Magical and wonderful. Hunter stood tall and gorgeous, and so alluring it made her ache to be closer to him.

I'd walk through miles of rain to get to him. Through fire, even, she thought with wonder.

It was like she was being compelled by some unseen force, more powerful than the pull of gravity. The fates, the Universe, the creators of it all had seemed to create this moment, this man, just for her. She was completely in awe of him.

"Hunter Maverick, this is Elissa Phoenix," Uncle Uzzi smiled.

"If I am not mistaken, *she* is your fated mate."

"*Elissa,*" Hunter said her name, drawing out each syllable as if he was making love to the word alone.

More moisture pooled between her legs. Elissa's heart thundered inside her chest and her pulse raced as intense need filled her.

"Well now, dear ones, I have to run. Elissa has agreed to stay on a few days to get acquainted. However, you don't own her, Mr. Maverick. Elissa is free to leave should she choose too. If this is not the right place for her, you will let her go."

"She will stay," he growled, his teal eyes never leaving Elissa's.

"Only if *she* chooses to," Uncle Uzzi agreed.

Elissa wished she could find her tongue, but she didn't seem capable of forming words at the moment. Her blood was pumping furiously in her veins, and breathing was taking up most of her thought process. Her body was reacting in a way she had never felt before.

Of course, she was not all that experienced with men. Not men like this, at any rate. Guys like Little Gianni seemed to be the only ones interested in her back home, but she'd always fantasized about someone who could make her feel like her body was about to explode with need.

Someone just like him.

It was not her fault, exactly. It was all those wonderful paranormal romance books she was always escaping into that gave her these false expectations of men.

Yay for book boyfriends!

But even her secret indulgence had not quite prepared her for the real thing. She could tell he was not the average man. Everything about him screamed he was special. And he was definitely that. Not just a Tiger Shifter, but the Neta of the entire Pride.

Elissa swallowed as a new rush of nerves

attacked her. What if she wasn't good enough for him?

"Alright, now I really have to run. Elissa, I have programmed my cell number into your phone. Don't be afraid to use it. And you, don't be a pussy when it comes to expressing your feelings. Elissa is a *normal*, she won't understand your grunting, chuffing, growling ways. Man up, and talk to her, yes? Good."

Elissa's eyes widened at the older Witch's frankness, but that was Uncle Uzzi for you. In the short time she'd known the remarkable man, she'd grown to trust him immensely. Elissa turned and hugged him impulsively.

"Oh, my! Okay yes, my dear," Uncle Uzzi said and hugged her back.

"You'll do, Elissa. You'll do just fine."

"Thank you," she whispered and bit her lip as Uncle Uzzi walked out of the room.

"So," she began, not knowing what to say.

"So," he mimed and smiled so wide, she was struck once more by his beauty.

He was beautiful. Manly, sexy, and powerful, too. She salivated just looking at him.

"Well, Elissa Phoenix, I believe Uncle Uzzi was right. I believe *you* are my fated mate," Hunter stated.

He crossed the space between them, but she'd

remained frozen in place. Everything about the way he moved made her aware of his presence. She recognized the power in that stride, and with every fiber of her being, she knew he would never harm a hair on her head.

His focus, so intense, so hot, and panty-melting, was on one thing only.

Her.

Elissa gasped, eyes wide. She'd never been lucky when it came to men. But something told Elissa her luck was about to change.

Yes, please.

Chapter Six

A few minutes earlier...

Hunter had heard the car as it rolled to a stop outside the Pride House. His sensitive ears told him the vehicle was not of his Pride.

Weird.

He wondered who would be coming to call on him on such a lousy night. It wasn't that it was terribly late, but the weather was too rough for friendly visits. Must be someone with an axe to grind.

Well, fuck.

He took a moment to prepare himself mentally for whatever was coming. As Neta, it was his duty to see to any perceived threats to his Pride. Hunter was responsible for the livelihoods and safety of about sixty individual Tiger adults. Some of them had families.

It wasn't very big, but that didn't matter. The Maverick Pride was his to take care of. Like it was his father's, grandfather's, and great-grandfather's before him. A Maverick had settled this land over two-hundred years ago, and one had run the Pride for just as long.

He was proud of his home, of his heritage. His father dying after he'd finished graduate school had been quite the shock, but Hunter had risen to the occasion. Taking over at the helm of Maverick Development and picking up as Neta where his father had left off, was not as hard a decision as some thought.

He was born to this. Had been raised to fill the old man's shoes. Fuck, he missed his dad. Grayson Maverick had been an excellent Neta. Even without his mother, who'd passed a long time ago, the old man had run the Pride and company as well as could be expected.

It was difficult for the Pride to lose their leader, but Hunter had been well received. And yes, he'd even offered them the ancient and seldom used *Rite to Challenge* ceremony before he ascended to the position.

There had been some who rose to the occasion. Hunter had to beat down a couple of younger Tigers looking to make names for themselves. Silly cubs, thinking him some soft city boy after his time at school.

But he'd proven himself then. And from time to time, he reminded his Tigers that he was the strongest among them. Their rightful leader. Their *Neta*.

Despite that, rumors popped up concerning his ability to rule. The latest ones claimed he was having problems controlling his beast. According to his nameless and faceless enemies, his lack of a mate would lead to his Tiger going rogue.

As if that bullshit wasn't bad enough, Hunter was having difficulty renewing Maverick Development's government contracts. The company supported the Pride, employing many of the able males and females.

Something was wrong, but he had his head turned in so many directions, Hunter could not focus. The local government was giving him shit, talking about lower bids coming in.

Un-fucking-believable.

This was his territory. The only other contractors stupid enough to poach it was a nearby Hyena Pack. Those fuckers had no real work ethic and a bad reputation. He'd need to have a meeting with the Alpha Fem of the Pack if they were thinking about challenging the Tiger Pride.

His ears perked up. The car had definitely stopped in front of the house. Just great. Now he needed to go see who this fucker was.

Hunter saved the spreadsheet he'd been working on and powered down his computer. Listening with his Tiger, he focused on the sound of unfamiliar voices. One was angry.

Blake, as usual.

He shook his head and stood up. Hunter wondered not for the first time if he'd made a mistake appointing his college buddy as his Beta when he'd come back home to Mount Maverick. He'd been emotional with the death of his only remaining parent and taking up the mantle of Neta had not come without challenges.

Tigers did not live in large groups like other Shifters. The Pride of his birth was small, with about less than sixty adult tigers all together. Living away from them while at school had been rough, but he knew it was necessary for him to develop the skills needed to run the company.

Money was a necessary evil, even for Shifters. Maverick Development was responsible for the well-being of the pride, and it needed to be solvent. Hell. It needed to be more than that.

The recent improvements to the homes and healthcare of members of his pride did not come cheap. But he wanted to be a good Neta, and caring for those men, women, and cubs was his honor and privilege.

Fucking Blake, he thought again when he heard the other man growling.

Blake Segal had been a loner when they met in college. He grew up in D.C. and was a single Tiger Shifter in a big city.

He'd been alone for some time. It struck Hunter as odd and a little sad when he'd met him. Shifters in the city tended to do poorly. Having no one to run with, no *Neta* to help control the animal within, made it difficult to blend with the humans around them.

Sometimes a Shifter went rogue, leaving the others no choice but to turn them in. A rogue Shifter was too dangerous to leave on his or her own and often, they would be hunted by the Council of Shifters.

That secret organization had representatives across Packs, Clans, and Prides. They created the laws which all agreed to abide by in order to keep the Shifter secret. Every Alpha, Neta, or Shifter group leader swore fealty to them when taking their position. Hunter had too, just like his father before him.

When Blake had asked him if they could team up together, Hunter had agreed. It seemed like the smart thing at the time, but just lately Blake had had trouble controlling himself. His angst was ramping up Hunter's own Tiger. Making it impossible for him to withstand the Shift for more than a week at a time.

Lately, it was even less than that. One of the Pride elders had suggested that having a mate would soothe his animal. That bit of advice had only spurred on new rumors that the Neta was losing his grip.

Hunter saw only one way to end the gossip. Finding his mate. It would squash those rumors questioning his ability to run the Pride and, on a personal note, he was ready to settle down.

Hunter wasn't opposed to the idea of a mate. Not

in the least. A woman around the place would be nice. One who could cook would be better.

Wow.

He ran his hands over the top of his shaved head. Hunter sounded like a chauvinistic asshole, even to himself. No wonder he was single.

Fine, he swore to readily admit to anyone who asked that he wanted a woman who would actually enjoy being his mate. Not some forced or arranged mating with a female Shifter who would sooner slice his balls off than fuck him.

No way did he want to deal with that. Hunter was a romantic at heart. He wanted a woman who was sweet, kind, who liked to cook, wanted to make love with him, and have his cubs.

Fuck yeah.

The thought of cubs made his Tiger chuff impatiently. The beast wanted young. So, yeah, that meant Hunter did too. But he couldn't be a dick about it.

It was the 21st century, for fuck's sake. Hunter might want a mate who could bear him many young, but he had to be open to her own plans and ideas. He knew this, and ideally, would not try to keep his mate tied down. But wouldn't it be nice if she wanted him and a family as much as he did?

Not that he thought women could only be wives and mothers. Just look at his sister. She ran her own business in town. Hunter simply didn't see himself with a career-oriented woman.

He was too possessive and demanding for that. Hunter wanted someone soft and pretty, who smelled good, who wanted to be the mother of his cubs.

Shit. Might as well throw in the towel now.

He was tired of eating what the unmated males in the Pride cooked nightly. The meat was either raw or burnt, unseasoned and bland. Fuck, nothing tasted good anymore.

The only time food was decent around the Pride House was on the nights Jessica cooked. She was a great sister, but she was no great cook. Her meals were merely edible in comparison to the crap the guys served.

Maybe he should just hire a damn chef instead of trying to find a mate who could cook? Might be easier. His cat scratched at him, and he sighed.

Okay, so he was intrigued with the notion of a mate. But Hunter didn't have time to sniff one out on his own. He knew none of the Pride females were his, so yes, he contacted *Uncle Uzzi's Magical Matchmaking Service* for help.

Uncle Uzzi had come highly recommended from the Pride elders. His parents had known the old Witch too. It seemed a win-win to Hunter. He'd be mated as soon as the busy dating guru could spare him some time.

Purrfect.

Besides, Hunter had to focus on renewing the contracts Maverick Development had with the surrounding counties and neighboring states to go traipsing about the country looking for a suitable mate.

With Uncle Uzzi on his side, he'd have a few weeks to finish fixing what was wrong with his bids, then he could turn his attention to sifting through the candidates the matchmaker would provide. Seemed easy enough.

That was his plan, at any rate. Fuck, he thought with a groan as he stretched. Being the Neta was not an easy job. This delay with their contracts had Hunter troubled. Maverick Development would be shit out of luck without them.

The company was not just the main source of income for the Pride. It was a good place allowing Shifters, who were renowned for their physical prowess, to work out their angst with physical labor. Started by his father more than eighty years ago, it was the best damn thing for the powerful Shifters who needed to expel their surpluses of energy.

Of course, Shifter longevity required some quick thinking on their part when it came to the books. It was a good thing Lance, one of the youngest Tiger Shifters in the Pride, was such a whiz on the computer, otherwise he wasn't sure how the Pride would maintain appearances.

Lance was responsible for making sure everyone had updated credentials, like birth certificates and licenses. Everything was carefully secured using the latest *Draco Fortis* firewall system. The Dragon run company was the best in supernatural software.

Damn, he was antsy. The voices from the other room were getting heated, and his Tiger growled deep in his chest. Hunter rolled his shoulders as he stared at the mountain of forms he still had to fill out.

If things didn't work out, they would need to find other sources of income. Tiger Shifters were notoriously reclusive. They did not play well with others, so finding outside work was the very last thing he wanted to do. As the Pride Neta, he could not let that happen.

Among the papers was yet another complaint from an employee about Blake. Seemed his Beta had been having difficulty managing his team when out on the job. They'd been accused of bullying some of their newer workers. It was the fifth time in three months Blake had started a disagreement.

Shit.

Bad enough Hunter had been forced to hire outside the Pride to level out the unevenness in the crew, but now he was thinking he had to demote his onetime best friend from foreman. Luckily, he'd found a widowed Bear Shifter from the nearby Barvale Clan a couple of months ago.

He'd been lumbering around the Pride territory when Hunter had picked up his scent. He'd sent him off with a single roar that the smart Bear took for the warning it was.

After that, the man had returned to Mount Maverick. He'd asked after Hunter, then he finally came to see him looking for work. It was an unusual thing for a Bear to be accepted into a Tiger Pride, but he was well-liked and respected by everyone far as Hunter could tell.

A perfect candidate to take on the role of foreman.

Brayden Smith was more than a decent man and Shifter. He was hardworking and tough as nails. A veritable fucking mountain. Quiet, punctual, and bigger than most of his Tigers, he'd earned a reputation for treating folks fairly.

Translation: he beat the shit out of the first few punks who thought they could take on the Black Bear and win.

Hunter grinned at the memory.

Good times.

Shifter fights were pretty common. They were a very physical group. Testing each other for dominance was inherent in their DNA. Of course, some felt fighting was beneath them, but they were a bunch of pansy asses, in Hunter's opinion.

Brayden was of the same opinion. Quiet didn't equal cowardly. The big Black Bear wasn't afraid to get down in the mud with the crew and other Pride members when necessary. Whether it was for work or play or just to blow off steam.

Now Blake, on the other hand, with his lazy city habits, would never even try to do half the work the Bear took on. It was becoming more and more apparent he was simply unfit for the job Hunter had given him.

Had he not been grieving for his lost parent, he would have come to another decision. He knew that now. But Blake had insisted he was the right man for the job, and Hunter had wanted him to be. That just reminded him of one of his mother's favorite sayings.

Sometimes all the wanting in the world doesn't mean a thing, son. It is your actions that define you.

It seemed no matter what Hunter told his old friend, Blake simply did not listen. He was determined to use his title as Beta to order others around.

Fuck.

His Tiger snarled, the beast uneasy for some reason. Hunter had dallied long enough. The raised voices and growls coming from the other room told him whoever his guests were, Blake was not happy to see them.

Fucking great. Another mess to clean up.

Chapter Seven

He stood up and opened the door to his office. It was one of the few rooms on the ground floor with an actual door that locked. A necessity when the house was full. Especially when he needed to get any work done.

Hunter frowned and turned down the hall. What was all the ruckus about? He breathed in deep and stopped dead.

Holy fuck.

Grrrrrrrrrrr.

Hunter felt as if he'd been sucker punched. Worse than that. It was like he'd been struck by lightning. He couldn't get any air into his lungs. Eyes watering, he gasped as the second breath he sucked in brought with it the heavenly scent. Something strange, but warm and decidedly feminine.

What is that scent?

Need it.

Want it.

Mine.

Grrr.

His Tiger snarled and scratched at his skin, urging the man to move closer to the owner of that fragrance. It was like fresh baked pie.

Cherry, he sniffed, *with a sugared crust. Yum.*

Hunter's favorite. A low rumble started deep in his gut. It built up to his chest, making his whole body vibrate. Need, want, and desire fought for dominance inside of him as he stealthily made his way to the large parlor.

Every step, every single breath he took, brought him closer to the source. He had to snag a mental leash around his Tiger to stop him from bursting through his skin, but the strong fucker continued to push and snarl.

The beast wanted him to stop fucking around already. He urged Hunter to run to the owner of the scent so he could finally breathe it from the source. And that wasn't all. The animal wanted to roll around in it. To taste it on his tongue.

Shit.

His cock hardened in his jeans, making it difficult to walk. He shook his head, trying to clear his mind, but that scent wrapped around him like a leash. Circling his body, his brain, his dick.

It tugged him forward, urging him to move, First one foot, then the other. He'd been doing this since he was a cub! He should be able to walk into a room without having to think through each step, but his brain was rapidly turning to mush. He was like one giant ball of need. But still, he inched his way there.

Pause. Sniff. Step. And repeat.

Finally, he stopped where the scent was strongest and took in the scene before him. Lust was the first emotion to hit him as he took in the short, curvy blonde who was holding her own against Blake.

The younger male was in her face, growling, it would seem. Unacceptable. Shifters did not intimidate females. Especially not this one, he thought with a growl of his own. What was even more astounding was the fact the tiny woman was standing up to his clearly agitated Beta.

That's when a second emotion hit him. Pure, unadulterated *rage*. What the fuck was Blake doing crowding his mate that way?

Mate?

He questioned his Tiger, pausing in his tracks.

Mate.

The animal growled back with barely leashed fury as he took in his supposed friend's threatening stance and leering smile.

He didn't need to ask his beast again. He accepted it for what it was. Fate. Destiny. Either word was fine. They could chat about it later. Only one thing mattered at that moment.

Her.

The beautiful stranger was his mate, and Blake was way too fucking close to her. Hunter was struck with the need to protect her. To get her to safety. He also had to work to not kill Blake for stepping to her that way.

Fuck that, snarled the beast.

His Tiger demanded he snap his Beta in two. This was not good. Hard to win a mate when you were covered in blood.

Who says, argued the beast. *She will know we can protect her.*

Hunter exhaled as he walked into the room. He allowed his powers as the Pride Neta to flow through him and press against the people inside the large living room. Just a little bit more of that natural or supernatural prowess was directed at his Beta.

Okay.

Maybe a whole lot more was directed at Blake, but Hunter was not about to apologize. The fucker clearly needed to be reminded that Hunter was in charge. And for the first time in a long time, this Pride Neta was more than happy to see to that himself.

Protect my Nari, his Tiger snarled and hissed the command.

Hunter moved faster, placing himself between the woman and his soon to be headless Beta.

Motherfucker, he thought with a sneer.

"Move."

That was it. One word. But within the word, his Tiger had embedded a very real threat. Blake, if he was smart, would do wise to listen. That word move meant the man was close to being permanently removed from this plane of existence.

Fucking, hell yes, he was. This was no threat. It was a promise.

If he did not move soon, Blake was going to have a brand-new second asshole. Somewhere right in the middle of his fucking stomach. A quick slice with

Hunter's right paw would open the tiny Tiger right up, spilling the fucker's guts onto the polished floor.

Yeah.

His beast liked that image. He growled long and hard at Blake, using only a hint more of his Neta power. It was all he could do not to lash out and rip the fucker's face off.

Mine.

Okay, so he was a possessive asshole.

Whatever.

The gorgeous creature behind him was his. Hunter would fucking destroy anyone who came close to even frowning at her, let alone piss and moan like this asshole had dared.

Later, he told his incensed beast. He'd carve Blake a new asshole later. After he introduced himself to the sweet female behind him.

That was if he could get beyond one-word sentences. Once Blake tucked tail and ran, Hunter turned to the blonde goddess.

"Who are you?" he asked.

Her large brown eyes blinked rapidly. He'd seen brown eyes aplenty, but none like hers. They were warm and translucent like really fucking good hundred- and sixty-year-old scotch. The kind he kept under lock and key to stop his men from getting their grubby paws on it.

Her eyes were like that, only better. Gorgeous and rare. A potent combination. And she would be his.

Mine. Grrr.

The beautiful woman bit her lip and swallowed hard.

Fuck, she was so tempting, and she didn't even realize it. Unlike any of the females of the Pride, this woman exuded grace and beauty, humility and passion, strength, and dignity all at once.

There were only three types of women he'd known in the past. The ones who'd flaunt themselves and beg him to service them during their heat. The ones too scared to even speak to him. And last, his sister.

That was it.

Shit.

Had he frightened her? He needed to try again.

"Your name," Hunter spoke again, taking special notice of her beautiful golden hair.

It was thick and long. Just how he liked it. He lifted a curl from her shoulder, noticing for the first time she appeared damp.

"Why are you wet?"

And why hasn't anyone given her a towel?

He turned his gaze and the young male who had followed behind him blanched and ran. Hopefully to get some fucking towels.

Fluffy warm ones.

He damn well better make sure they were soft and freshly laundered or there'd be hell to pay. What the hell had everyone been doing while his mate shivered and shook?

Couldn't they see his *Nari* was wet from the rain? He needed to help her. To dry her or something. Get her warm. Of course, that sent images of all the delightful ways he could warm her sifting through his mind.

Oh yeah, he could warm her up just right.

He imagined peeling those damp clothes off until she was nude with just his body to heat her. It sent a wave of lust right to his cock making his jeans uncomfortably tight. His Tiger wholeheartedly agreed with the plan.

Take her to bed. Claim her. Mine.

His thoughts were interrupted by a fierce little Witch with a mighty strong poke.

Shit.

Embarrassment burned his cheeks as Mr. Stregovich, the old matchmaking Witch, reminded him he was the Neta of the Maverick Pride, not some unlicked cub. He knew better than to behave this way.

"Do you want to stay?" Uncle Uzzi asked Elissa in their supposed private conversation.

Hunter heard every word, of course. He tensed. She had to stay. She was his. But what if she didn't want to? Fear made his mouth dry. He was not used to feeling that particular emotion, and he had to admit, it felt like shit.

Of course, Uncle Uzzi knew he could hear what they were saying. The wily old Witch made it clear the female was in charge. As it should be, he agreed.

Hunter hadn't meant to listen, but he had no choice. He was ready to butt in and demand she never leave, but it seemed he didn't have to. Relief poured through him at her acquiescence.

Purrfect.

Chapter Eight

Hunter's beast was overjoyed that his little mate felt their connection.

Yes.

It would make wooing that much easier. And he really wanted to get it right. He had no idea asking Uncle Uzzi to find his mate would lead to this kind of mind leveling certainty that nothing would ever be the same again.

All he wanted was to gather her in his arms and rub his scent all over her body. To mark her, claim her, make sure everyone knew who she belonged to.

He wanted to tear the clothes from her body and bury himself balls deep in her wet heat. And yes, she was wet. Fuck yeah. He'd caught the scent of her arousal earlier and it almost sent him crashing to his knees.

As Uncle Uzzi said his goodbyes, Hunter walked over to her. Careful not to upset or frighten his lovely *Nari*.

She was so small compared to him. He frowned, hoping she wasn't too put off by his appearance. She was so beautiful and petite.

Hunter was a big fucking guy. Six-foot six-inches and two hundred ninety-five pounds of pure, hard muscle. With his shaved head and intense stare, he knew he scared the shit out of most guys.

Purrfect for the Pride Neta. Not so great when you were trying to seduce a woman into being your mate.

Fucking hell.

Hunter needed her to agree to stay with him forever. Once he gave her his claiming bite, there was no telling if it would awaken an animal within her or not.

Fuck, he hadn't thought of that. It was exceedingly rare, but Pride members still whispered about it. They referred to the process as the *Puspa*.

It occurred when a Tiger Shifter took a *normal* or human as a mate. During the claiming, that was

Shifter speak for sex with some biting and scratching, the Shifter sometimes woke the *animal within* the normal.

It did not happen with every mate. In fact, it was highly unusual, almost unheard of for a mate to experience the *Puspa* in this day and age.

Hunter didn't give a fuck. *Normal* or *Shifter*, he wanted her and only her. Elissa Phoenix, delicate female, curvy temptress, was everything he ever wanted.

And he didn't know a thing about her, he thought with a laugh. Didn't matter. She was his. Elissa was it for him.

Every cell in his body thrummed with the knowledge that in front of him was the only woman who would ever occupy that special place in his life. She was the only other person in the world who mattered. At least until she had his cubs.

Cubs.

Now it was his turn to swallow hard. The image of her swollen with his young had him growing even harder in his too tight jeans, if that was even possible.

Slow it down.

Even if they were blessed enough to experience

the *Puspa*, she wasn't a Shifter now. She was a *normal,* and he needed to explain some things to her.

Fuck.

It had been so long since he'd been out in the *normal* world. He didn't know where to start. Now that he was in charge of Maverick Development, he spent more time in the office than out with the crews. A change he didn't relish.

Until now.

It would give him more time with his Nari, and it would allow him to make the necessary adjustments within the Pride. Things he'd been putting off. Like setting Blake straight. But first things first.

"So, *Elissa*, I believe Uncle Uzzi is right. I believe you are my mate," he stated slowly.

He figured it was best to lead with the truth. He had no intention of lying to her. He could never do that.

Not ever.

Hunter had been waiting for his entire life for this moment, whether he knew it or not. He would always treat her well. She was precious.

Purrfect.

Mine.

E lissa swallowed.
Hard.
"Mate? Well, um," she said idiotically.

"Uncle Uzzi mentioned that might be a possibility when he drove me here," Elissa finished her thoughts in a husky voice she hardly recognized as hers.

"Here," Hunter said, handing her the fluffy white towel some young man brought him.

She'd noticed the guy earlier as he'd followed Hunter into the room. One look from Hunter, and the male had run off to grab the freshly dried towel before returning with it. He'd held it out to his Neta, without looking directly at him.

Neta, she thought, mulling the word over. It sounded foreign when she first heard it from Mr. Stregovich, but now it seemed to fit the man standing before her.

The other male was no more than twenty. A baby really, but he was already stunningly handsome like all the men she'd seen so far. He smiled shyly and waved, backing off quickly when Hunter glared at him.

Elissa frowned. Was he mean to all kids? Sex appeal or not, she couldn't condone bullying of any kind. He seemed to note her displeasure and closed his eyes as if trying to wrestle down his aggression.

That was nice. At least he was trying. But she'd have to watch out for that kind of behavior.

"Here, why don't we find you something dry to wear?"

He cocked his head to the side, reminding her of the cat she used to feed outside her apartment when she was a kid.

It had belonged to the neighborhood bakery. A sly old tabby with huge orange eyes. He'd learned quickly that if he came around to Elissa's window on Fridays during Lent, he would get the tuna fish on whole wheat she'd secretly loathed.

Her grandmother made it for her every week just before Easter, and every week, Elissa fed it to the cat instead of toting it all the way to school. She hadn't wanted to hurt the older woman's feelings by telling her she didn't like it.

As far as Grandma knew, Elissa loved everything she'd ever made. And that was just fine with her.

It was so weird to think this handsome, virile man could turn into an enormous Tiger. He seemed to vibrate with energy and power. His entire demeanor was one of authority. She had to admit, it was attractive.

She wasn't going to start this thing with a lie. Not about that. But there were a lot of things Elissa did not know or understand. She was completely new to this world.

A shiver ran through her, and Elissa realized she was feeling pretty icky in her wet clothes.

Wow.

Her date with Gianni seemed like a lifetime ago. And it was merely hours. She should really call Gretchen, but later. It was like she was in some alternate reality now and she didn't want her time there to end.

Maybe this is my new reality, she thought to herself.

"What was that?" he asked.

"Oh, nothing," she replied.

Elissa followed Hunter up a wide staircase to a second level of rooms. He turned right, then left. The place was large, but it was pretty straightforward. Simply decorated with highly polished wood floors and sturdy looking furniture.

No photos graced the walls, but there were what looked like hand carved figures of Tigers, Bears, and Wolves on the shelves and side tables. Tall potted trees sat near the enormous windows, and there were skylights every few feet.

She wondered how they would look on clear nights. Would the moonlight filter through and make everything seem even more Magical than it already did?

She sighed and continued to follow, taking in the clean lines and simple decor. Everything was painted in muted colors, but it was nice and neat. She liked that, appreciated it even. Suddenly, she was in what looked like an entire wing of private rooms.

His private rooms, she was certain. These were cut off from the rest of the Pride House.

Totally private.

It was apart from the others, like a townhouse, she thought. Elissa swallowed as she realized they were truly alone in this section.

Just the two of them.

Need and desire wrapped around her like a blanket. Anticipation made her shiver and tingle with each step she took. She wasn't sure what was going to happen, but something was surely about to go down.

Hopefully, it would be him. She blushed at her own needy thoughts. Her sex throbbed, lips moistened, and for once in her life, she was almost tempted to make the first move.

Naughty girl.

Was she wrong? She didn't think so. She simply couldn't imagine Hunter Maverick, Pride Neta, taking her to his rooms unless it was so he could have his wicked way with her.

Yes, please.

She bit her lip as she pictured all the ways he could make each and every one of her fantasies come to life. Shocked at the deep, sexual attraction she felt for the stranger, what was even more odd was the way her heart seemed to stop every time his icy teal eyes found hers.

He was so unbelievably sexy. The moisture dripping between her legs was proof of that. When had a man, any man, ever gotten her so hot and ready?

He stopped in his tracks, and she almost bumped right into his back. He breathed deep and let out a long rumbling growl that seemed to send bolts of need straight to her sex.

Uh oh.

Hadn't Uncle Uzzi warned her Shifters could scent things like desire? She better put a damper on those kinds of thoughts.

Focus on the rooms instead, she told herself.

They were quite nice. Done in cool greens and tans. It sort of reminded her of a forest. She could almost imagine his Tiger slinking through, undetected, ready to pounce on some unsuspecting bit of prey.

Ooh yes, please let it be me.

Chapter Nine

She squeaked when he took up his pace again, only to stop suddenly right in front of her. Too late for her to slow her steps, Elissa walked right into his back.

His big, sexy, muscular back that smelled of something spicy and delicious.

"*Oof*," she groaned, but smiled when he turned and warm hands touched her shoulders, steadying her.

"You okay?" he asked, his eyes warming with concern.

Elissa nodded her reply. His thumbs were moving in tiny little circles on the sleeves of her damp blouse, creating little infernos along her skin through the thin fabric.

That's kind of nice, she thought.

Elissa leaned into the touch, loving the sensations he was causing. She whimpered when he withdrew his hands and stepped a couple of feet away. He opened a solid wooden door to reveal an enormous bathroom.

"In here."

She marveled at the size of the bathroom. Heck, it was bigger than her bedroom back home. Dark blue tiles lined the floors and the walls, a sunken tub sat in the center, and a glass enclosed shower was off to the left.

It was big and expensive looking. A luxury she would love to indulge in.

With him.

Would he want to share a bath with her? Did mates do things like that? Her thoughts were positively x rated as far as the man standing next to her was concerned. Still, she couldn't seem to stop.

Hunter was like a walking, talking fantasy come to life. She just had to look at him and the images of him and her doing the nasty were set to permanent replay, for fuck's sake.

All that delicious muscle and smooth tanned skin. He was breathtaking. What would it feel like to slide into that tub knowing he was waiting in the depths of that warm water just for her?

Her stomach tightened. She might as well just throw her panties away. Like all of them. What was the point? They would never stay dry around him.

That was assuming he meant it when he'd said she was his mate. Who could be sure? Not her. She was used to being in the friend zone for any of the really good-looking guys she knew. Not that they were in his league.

Neither was she, for that matter. Chubby and cute, sure. But streamlined and gorgeous? She most definitely was not. Hunter was like the blessed offspring of a supermodel and a professional football player, only hotter. *Way hotter.*

He had more going for him than any one man she'd ever seen. What was he doing contacting a matchmaking service? Even a Magical one.

She sure as hell didn't know, but she was glad. Otherwise, she might never have laid eyes on him.

Whoa. Was it getting warm in here?

The sound of a rumbling growl met her ears. When she looked at him, she noted he'd moved closer once again. Just a step, but it was enough for her to feel the heat radiating from his body.

Gulp.

His eyes were glowing, a lightning thin line of gold rimmed the translucent teal.

Was that his Tiger?

Oh my.

Gulp again.

She watched him inhale the air around her deeply. His big body tensed, but he never broke eye contact. He watched her, like a cat eyeing a mouse. A mouse he wanted to eat.

Here kitty.

Clearing her throat, she took a step back. Hunter followed, nodding his head at the tub and shower stalls. She noticed the way he clenched and unclenched his fists.

Like he was trying to regain some semblance of control. She liked that. Knowing she threw him off balance was a rush. A totally hot one.

Elissa had never had that kind of power. She bit her lip, wondering how far to pursue this newfound discovery. It made her bold, daring thoughts filled her. Would it be wise to touch him? Was she allowed to?

"Please help yourself to a warm bath if you like. There's soap and shampoo in the dispenser. Towels and a bathrobe are in the closet," he pointed to a cabinet and went to the door.

"Hunter?"

"Yes?"

"Thank you."

"You don't have to thank me for taking care of you. It is my privilege."

Well, day-um.

That was unexpected. She'd been prepared for the sexy, but not the heart melting sweetness. Elissa felt herself grow warm from the inside out.

Her damp clothes and the state of her hair forgotten. Were there even men left in the world who said things like that to women? Apparently, there was one. And if this was real, he was hers.

That is, *if* she believed Mr. Stregovich's claims. Maybe she should, after all. What did she have to lose?

Only your heart, Lissa. Only your heart.

Before she could lose herself in her thoughts and nagging doubts, he spoke again. The sound of that deep, rumbling voice met her ears, and she sighed. She could listen to him all day long.

"Elissa, I know we're strangers and this whole thing has been kind of sudden, but you can trust me. I swear, I will always tell you the truth."

She swallowed hard. Might as well test him now and find out if he was trustworthy.

C.D. GORRI

"Can I ask you something, Hunter?"

"Anything," his voice was deep and low.

Glowing teal eyes raked over her body, she knew her top was clinging to her breasts because of the rain, and normally, she'd shy away from anyone who stared.

But Elissa liked his eyes on her. She enjoyed knowing the flare of his nostrils and licking of his lips was because of her. It did wonderful things to her self-confidence, knowing he wanted her.

Maybe she was foolish, but for the first time in forever, Elissa wanted to throw caution to the wind. Tired of always doing the right thing. The expected thing. The boring thing.

She wanted to take a leap of faith, like Uncle Uzzi had said. She wanted to jump right into the deep end.

With him.

"Hunter, what does it mean to be your mate?"

She took one step closer to him, then another.

"It means, uh," he breathed deep.

He is scenting me, she thought.

The act itself was hot, and more moisture leaked from her needy sex. She bit her lip. Now he would know just how desperate she was for his touch.

Oh well. She never was the kind to hide her

emotions. Elissa watched him open his mouth, pink tongue dart out as if he was tasting her on the air itself.

Good, she grinned. She wanted him to know how much she wanted him. She wanted him to want her back.

His eyes glittered and chest rumbled as she bent forward, tops of her breasts practically hitting the floor as she slipped off her shoes. Hunter cleared his throat.

"Hunter?" she reminded him of her question. This teasing side of her was new, and she welcomed it, wanted to explore it with him.

"It means that you are mine," he growled, eyes flashing at her.

"You were created, *fated* if you will, just for me."

Well, double day-um.

That was so hot. Elissa licked her suddenly dry lips, and he groaned with the action. He stepped closer, nuzzling her cheek with his and sucking in more of her scent. Fuck, she was desperate for his lips, his touch, anything he would give her. Desire swelled between them, so thick, she was oblivious to everything but him.

"I am the only one who can soothe that ache inside you, *Nari*," he growled the words.

"What does that mean?"

"It means, my queen," he told her.

"But what about me? What do I mean to you?" Elissa asked, betraying her secret doubts to him with those two questions.

She paused, waiting for some hint of cruelty or judgment. Only it never came.

Thank fuck.

Hunter cupped her face with his hands and lifted until she was forced to look at him. This close, the man was devastatingly handsome. So much so, she was pretty damn sure she was about to go up in flames from that one look.

"Elissa Phoenix, when I call you Nari, when I claim you are my mate, I am telling you that you, my beautiful female, are the single most important person in my life."

Holy. Fuck.

"Okay then," she replied.

Elissa could so live with that. If anyone else in the world had said that she would've scoffed at them. Actually, she'd probably have already told them off for talking shit to her.

Trust came hard for Elissa, but for some reason, one she could barely believe, she wanted to believe.

She trusted this stranger. It was like her heart recognized him.

I think I might love him already, she mused, surprising herself.

All her doubts fell away as she leaned forward, and he stepped back once, then twice. Hunter followed her with his gaze, but he'd retreated. That was funny.

He stilled a few steps away, like a giant, sexy statue. She knew those wonderful muscles of his were ready to pounce. It was as if he was waiting for her to attack. The irony of it made her grin. He was a big, bad Tiger, but it was *she* who was stalking the predator.

"What else?" she asked as her hands went to the waistband of her leggings.

Teal eyes followed her movements with laser-like precision. Slowly, Elissa pushed the damp material over her wide hips and down her legs.

Normally, she'd be panicked by now. Her thighs were too big, her legs too short, but if what he'd said was true, he wouldn't mind.

No, I'm not going there tonight.

She pushed away all negative thoughts. If she was his mate, he needed to see the real her before they went any further. Plump belly, round hips, thick thighs, large boobs, jiggly ass, and all.

No lies or misconceptions. She was who she was, and Elissa was a big girl. She'd make no apologies. Not now that he'd said she was his mate.

Better know what he was getting himself into now. She steeled herself for his cold rejection, surprised when the heat in his eyes declared anything but.

Judging from the sound building in his massive chest, Hunter didn't mind her curves. Not one little itty bitty bit.

Her long top covered her private bits, but just the hint of her skin seemed to tempt him. His Tiger looked as if he wanted to come out and play, too. Gold rimmed eyes bore into hers.

"I said, what else?" she repeated, pausing with her hands on the hem of her tunic.

She might not be a Shifter, but she felt desire rise between them. Sensed it in the air. The large bathroom practically sizzled with the energy flowing between her and the big Tiger.

"Just what I said. You are mine. Only you. No one else. Not ever."

"Yeah?"

"Yesssss," he hissed, his control waning.

"You belong to me."

"What if someone else comes along for you or me?" she asked.

"No," he shook his head, baring his teeth.

"No other males. Mine," he growled.

Fuck. That was so damn hot.

She noted his eyes were pure gold now and he was trembling with either desire or anger. Maybe a bit of both.

Uncle Uzzi did mention Shifters had a wildly jealous streak.

"If I belong to you, what are you gonna do about it?"

"Mate you. Claim you. Fuck you. Now."

Elissa straightened her shoulders. Her hands going slowly towards the buttons of her tunic.

"*Purrfect*," he grunted, as she revealed more and more of her skin to his glowing gaze.

"Lissa, it's killing me to say this, but if you don't want me to do something about this right now, I think I should leave."

"What if I do want you to do something?" she asked, standing so close to him now she could feel his warm breath on her forehead.

For the first time in a long time, she felt sexy and wanted. There was power and beauty in that, but also something else. Her heart swelled and her body responded to the need she saw burning for her in his beautiful, glowing eyes.

A Shifter. A real honest to God Shifter. And he was hers. Her mate. She belonged to him, and he to her.

She just needed to let it happen.

Chapter Ten

Thunder roared in his brain. The sexy temptress was teasing him to within an inch of his sanity. He was desperate to touch her, hold her, fuck, he needed her.

But acting like a possessive caveman wasn't going to win him any favors. He had to rein in his beast. But she was doing things to him, he never thought possible. Then, when he thought he couldn't take it anymore. She gave him hope.

Grrrrrrr.

His Tiger growled, ready to move in. But Hunter couldn't believe his ears. Was Elissa really ready for him to claim her?

It sure seemed that way. But there was so much

he had not told her yet. Maybe he didn't have to. Maybe Uncle Uzzi had covered everything?

Fuck.

Hunter couldn't keep his thoughts organized. His sexy as hell mate was doing a slow striptease for him, and he was about to lose his damn mind. With every delectable inch of creamy pale skin she uncovered, he lost more of his brain cells.

"Are you sure?" he asked.

His Tiger snarled inside his mind's eye. The beast tensed as he waited on the metaphysical plane of reality where his animal half resided until they swapped skins.

The beast wanted to take a bite out of his human half's ass for slowing things down. His Tiger was all about pouncing on his delectable mate and claiming her right now.

Images of his human side flipping her over, taking her from behind and sinking his teeth into her flesh, filled his brain.

That would be just purrfect, thought his horny as fuck Tiger.

Fuck, his cat was actually purring. Had been since he'd seen her, he realized.

Tigers don't fucking purr.

Well, they did now. His Tiger was sure as shit fucking purring at this very moment.

Shit.

His dick throbbed as she slowly released her glorious long hair from its constrictive ponytail. He wanted to wrap it around his fist and yank her back for a kiss, smack that fine ass while filling her pretty pussy. Mark her with his cum. Get his scent all over her. Inside her too. Then he'd place his bite right there on the smooth skin of her shoulder.

Fuck yeah.

That sounded like a plan. Long, sharp claws threatened to push through his fingertips. His gums ached with the need to descend his fangs. It was his beast making himself known. The Tiger wanted to claim the female. To mark her with his seed, claws, and teeth.

Fuck. Just breathe.

Hunter knew he needed to tone it down. He didn't want to hurt his mate. But she was so frail, so precious. She was a normal and not used to their ways.

We would never hurt her.

He knew that, but still. What if he was too rough? Hunter had been with human females, but not since he was younger.

Like most Shifters, he did not like to hold back during intercourse. The females he'd bedded knew the deal. They enjoyed it rough, raw, and dirty. No judgements and pleasure guaranteed for all involved.

That was all fine, and good, but this was his mate. His very beautiful, very human mate. Hunter needed to treat her gently this first time. He was a big male all over, and he meant that without conceit.

She was so tiny, so fragile. Knowing this, he had to proceed slowly and with care. To ease her into accepting him physically. Not easy when the ways he and his beast wanted to have her kept playing over and over in his head like some XXX porn marathon.

Fuck.

His human side grabbed his Tiger by the ruff. Hunter gave him a single, hard shake. He needed to take care. He reminded his animal that his mate was a normal.

He inhaled, savoring more of her delicious cherry pie scent, and looked into her soft brown eyes. She was ripe and ready, Hunter needn't worry. He could tell from her scent and that sexy, heavy-lidded stare.

Yes. This was the right time, and it would be good. He would always go at her pace, the Tiger, and the man in complete agreement that her pleasure came first.

Always.

Puspa, the beast hissed the word at him.

Hunter went still. He understood what the animal wanted. To give his mate more than the claiming mark, to give her the bite that would change her irrevocably.

The Puspa only happened if the Fates allowed. When everything lined up correctly between a Shifter and his or her mate. Then and only then. Wouldn't that be incredible? But only as a bonus. Elissa was the real treasure. Shifter or not.

Doesn't matter. We will go slow to prove our worth. To show our unwavering devotion. To make her feel our love. We will fulfill her every dream until she believes it down to the depths of her soul.

The animal grumbled but agreed with Hunter's plan. Ultimately, the Tiger wanted his human side to claim her.

Whatever it takes.

He looked up to tell her so, and his mouth went dry. In the moments he'd taken to gain control of his beast, his beautiful Nari had dropped her shirt. Bold and beautiful, Elissa stood before him, nearly naked.

Her chin jutted out proudly, trepidation in her

gorgeous brown eyes. Beast and man stuttered at the mere sight of her. She had every right to be proud. His Nari was a goddess.

Holy shit.

Hunter didn't know what to expect, but he thanked the gods now for gifting him such an exquisite creature. She trembled slightly, and he realized he had yet to react. Her tiny hands fisted at her sides. Determined now, he licked his dry lips.

Elissa was wearing a skimpy pair of bubblegum pink briefs with a matching bra that left the creamy tops of her breasts almost bare for him. Her ample bosoms rose and fell with every breath she took, giving him an even better view of her assets.

His mouth watered, and his cock ached. She was exquisite. Soft and rounded, more than a handful, even for him. And Hunter had big fucking hands.

The sound of her breathing teased his sensitive ears and he savored it. She was fucking *purrfect*.

Prrrrrrrrrrrrrrrrrrrrrrrrrrrrrrrrr.

All of his blood seemed to divert to his cock, and Hunter was left speechless, unable to do anything but breathe along with her. Her sumptuous scent filled his nostrils and he salivated. A nice word for what he really did. Hunter actually fucking drooled.

Fuck.

He wiped his mouth as casually as he could. Feeling like a fucking idiot, but what could he do? She was amazing. Smiling shyly, his sweet mate moved forward and pressed herself against him. Her soft hands lifted to cup his face, and she tugged him forward in a move he found sexy as hell.

Aggressive women were not his thing, but when it was his mate who showed him how much she wanted him, all bets were off. Fuck, he would do anything to please her. Anything at all.

He followed her lead, letting her pull his head down until they were face to face. He could hardly breathe for wanting her. Like a man in a trance, he waited for her to make the first move. And she did.

Thank the Fates themselves.

Her soft lips touched his, shyly at first. Hunter gasped, completely unprepared for the spark, that feeling like he was suddenly alive again after a lifetime of being half-asleep, to spike through his veins. He was not prepared for the avalanche of need that accompanied the brief meeting of their lips.

One kiss.

That's all it was, and yet it was so much more than that. It was like a cataclysmic collision of two entirely separate worlds. That one touch created a force so strong and powerful it swept everything else away with the power of its explosion.

All the things Hunter had ever thought he'd known about life, his Pride, himself, were now null and void. Nothing else mattered. Nothing even existed before her.

No other female. Hell, no other person. His entire world became Elissa Phoenix in that moment when he'd felt her lips on his.

She was his. His Nari. And he was going to keep her.

Mine.

His Tiger bellowed the word in a deafening roar. He was sure the rest of the Pride felt the beast's claim through the ancient and Magical bonds that held them together.

Good, snarled his Tiger.

The Pride would know their Nari. They would protect and serve her as they did him. She was their future. She would carry the new generation in her womb. His mate.

Mine.

Roarrrrrr.

Growling deep in his throat, Hunter sucked on her tongue, loving the contradictions in her sweet and spicy feminine flavor. The richness of it burst along his taste buds, making him want her all the more.

He wrapped his big arms around his almost naked mate and pulled her to him. He wanted her to carry his scent. Needed her to wear it on her skin.

It was another aftereffect of their mating. She would have his scent on her and he would carry hers with him. A sign that they belonged to each other.

Always.

Their kiss deepened, and Hunter left all logic behind. He licked her lips, sucking on her tongue and exploring every last detail of her heavenly mouth.

Mmm. She really is sweet as cherry pie.

Her skin was still chilled from her damp clothing, but he wasn't worried. He knew just how to warm her up. His tiger chuffed, the beast within him urging him on. But Hunter did not need any urging.

He was already head over heels for the female. Breathing erratically, he pulled her in tight, loving the feel of her softness against his muscled frame. She was short, but that was no problem, he growled and lifted her, loving the way she squeaked in surprise.

More. Want more, no, I need more, he thought.

"Hunter," she mewled his name.

Her soft moans and pants as he nuzzled her ears, and neck drove him wild. Finally, he made his way back to her sweet lips, pressing his to hers in an urgency he could only just begin to understand. Fuck, she was beautiful, and he was desperate for her.

He met her breathy pleas with his mouth, hands, and tongue. Knowing she wanted him was better than an aphrodisiac, and her soft hands were making him crazy. She ran them over his head and neck, pulling him closer.

The bite of her blunt fingernails as she increased the pressure made his Tiger growl appreciatively. His sweet Elissa needn't worry about hurting him. He was strong. He could take anything she dished out.

Yessss, hissed his Tiger.

As if to prove it, he urged her on. Grunting approvingly as she clawed at his shoulders and back. His hands traced the underside of her breasts. The soft swells were smooth as silk, warm and heavy in his palm as he cupped and weighed one then the other, kissing her all the while.

Elissa moaned and scratched at his shoulders, but damn, he loved that hint of pain. Hunter was one big ball of need. He was aching with anticipation. The urge to cherish the woman whose mouth he was plundering nearly sent him to his knees.

More.

Mine.

All.

Fuck, he was shaking like a cub. He needed more than this. The beast inside of him demanded it.

"Please," Elissa murmured against his lips and that was when Hunter stopped fucking around.

Her whimpers grew louder as he dove headfirst into their kiss. She moaned his name, urging him on. When her fingers skimmed over his head, he tensed. He'd never thought about whether or not women liked his shaved head. He just hated hair. It got in the fucking way and was easier to care for like this.

He was the Neta. He had no time to mess around with girly fucking hair products like some of his Pride. It was a damn embarrassment if you asked him.

Grown ass men fucking around with shit with foody names like gel and mousse. The only mousse he wanted near him was the chocolate kind. With whipped cream.

Ooh. Whipped cream.

The fun he could have with his sexy little mate and a can of the creamy white stuff.

Grrr.

Not that he needed any enticement to lick her from head to toe. Her cream was more than enough for him.

Fuck yeah.

Hair or his lack thereof had never mattered to him before. In fact, he'd never even questioned his decision to open a pack of razors and go to town on his skull every other day. But suddenly he did care, very much about what she thought.

Hunter only wanted to make her happy. He wanted that with every fiber of his being. If she wanted him to grow his hair, he would. Down to his fucking knees if need be. But he'd ask her about it later. Much later.

Elissa wiggled her hips to fit herself more closely to him, and the bar of his cock nestled against the hot apex of her thighs. Her legs wrapped around him as they made out like teenagers, but better. He knew what he was doing now, whereas teen Hunter would have already come inside his tighty-whities.

He sucked on her tongue, his hands tracing over her silky skin, memorizing every curve and dip of her incredible body. He couldn't wait to lose himself inside of her. But only when she was ready for him.

He needed her primed to accept him and his mating mark.

Yes, the Tiger agreed.

He had to show her without words just what he was going to do to her body. He wasn't big on talking about his feelings. Where words could only fail him, actions had always proven best. His hands held onto the round globes of her peach-shaped ass, and Hunter walked them over to the sunken tub. A flick of the handle had it filling with water while he shucked off his clothing.

Never once did he put her down or stop kissing her. He didn't have to, he yanked off the bothersome clothes, ripping where necessary until he was naked as the day he'd been born.

This was it.

The most important moment of his entire life. Grabbing the edges of her panties, he stopped, slowing his kiss before going further.

"Are you partial to these?" he asked.

"Hmm? Oh, not really," she said, biting her lower lip.

"Good."

Purrrrrrrrrrrrrrrrr.

Chapter Eleven

"Are you sure about this? There is no going back once we do this," he explained, offering one last chance to refuse.

He didn't know how he would survive if she walked out now, but the choice was hers. Always.

"I'm sure," she replied, her voice husky with need.

Hunter held Elissa's curious lust filled gaze as his fingers lengthened to claws. Her surprised gasp was rough and hypnotic. His beast wanted more of that sound. And he wanted it now. The predator inside of him growled low in his chest as he sliced through the elastic waistband and tore the flimsy fabric from her supple hips.

Using more care with her bra, Hunter's claws receded. With human hands once more, he released the clasp between her precious breasts. His claws would never go near her supple skin. Oh no, Hunter never wanted to hurt his delicate mate in any way.

Only pleasure, never pain. The sight of her bare breasts stole his breath. Her creamy round globes filled his hands. The abundant flesh spilling over, and this time he was the one who groaned.

So fucking good, he thought as he gathered them to his mouth.

Licking and suckling one than the other, Hunter wanted to devour her. Her body was a glorious feast, but only for him.

So sweet.

So delicious.

So mine.

"Hunter," she cried his name.

Yes, call my name, he wanted to roar, but a grunt was all he could utter in reply. It was the only name she'd call out from now on.

He wanted to hear it again. Vowed to make her scream it when he filled her hot little pussy and drove home until she clenched around his cock and came again and again.

"Wanna fill you, mate," he said, telling her exactly what he wanted to do to her.

He scented her arousal, growled as her need

spiked with his words. She liked it when he talked dirty, so Hunter kept on whispering naughty little things as he lifted her once more.

"Wanna feel your pussy tight around my cock, mate. Gonna stretch your tight sheath, fill you up with my cock. Feel how hard I am for you? I can't wait till I'm buried inside you. Gonna stroke you so good. Gonna please my mate," he growled.

Then Hunter lifted her hips, his mouth smashed to hers as he settled her astride his legs. The warm water rose and splashed with the movement, and her moan told him she was much more comfortable now than she had been freezing in his living room before.

His animal was frustrated. It had taken him so long to care for his mate, but Hunter ignored the beast. His attention on the woman whose pussy was resting atop his needy cock.

She moaned and flexed her hips, sliding her wet heat along his girthy member. She writhed and moaned, no passive observer to their lovemaking.

Not his Elissa. Oh no, his mate was wild and fierce, clinging to him and running her small hands over his body. She approved of him in that way at least. The rest would have to wait.

His ass was on the marble seat inside the tub, built specifically with this activity in mind. Hunter was grateful he'd waited for her to experience this bit of erotic play.

Like so many things inside the Pride House, he'd designed and built it with a mate in mind. His Tiger had been urging him towards claiming one for years. But there could never be anyone for him, save Elissa Phoenix.

His heart thudded unsteadily in his chest as he lifted her sweet, curvy body so that her legs spread even wider. Fuck, she was so soft, so warm. Hunter gripped her hips firmly.

Warm water swirled all around them, moving frantically with the jets inside the tub, but Hunter was oblivious to all of it. Elissa was his only focus. She was all he could see, touch, taste, and feel. Her pleasure, her emotions, everything she was experiencing were right there for him to witness. Etched in her expressions, reflected in her moans and pants, and Hunter wanted to savor them all.

"You feel like silk," he whispered, licking a trail from her earlobe to her remarkable cleavage.

"And you feel incredible, Hunter," she replied. "So hard, so good."

"You're tight, baby, so tight. I'll go slow," he said on a growl.

She moved her hips, placing her wet heat over his

cock and using a downward flex, his sexy seductress pressed down onto his cock. She tensed, his mushroomed head pressing just inside her slick folds.

Fuck, her pussy was so hot, so tight, and it made him even harder, if that was even fucking possible. All he wanted was to thrust forward and enter her slick heat in one solid motion, burying himself to the hilt inside her. The Tiger agreed, wanting his human half to claim his *Nari* and roar his completion to one and all.

Not yet.

He was barely able to hold on, but he did. He would never take his pleasure at the expense of hers. No, he needed to give her time. Besides, it would be over far too soon if he sunk into her sweet sex to the hilt now.

He had other things in mind for her first. Hunter nipped her lower lip and fisted her long blonde hair. He pulled her head back gently but firmly, so that he could lick along her neck down to her pretty pink-tipped breasts.

Her nipples were hard with her arousal. Plump cherries ripe for his lips. The dusky color circling her nubs was gorgeous, just like everything else about her. He licked and fondled, drawing torturous little moans from her mouth.

Pinching one bud and suckling the other, he noted the increase in her breathing. Mouth open, she panted, pushing her chest out to entice him further, opening her legs even wider, and taking him deeper into her incredible body.

Fuck yes.

His sexy as hell mate liked it when he used his teeth, and Hunter was more than happy to oblige. He'd lick and nibble every sumptuous inch of her if she'd let him. A slave to her desire, he would do anything and everything for her.

Her pleasure was his only goal. His ultimate goal. Whatever else he was, Neta, Tiger, son, brother, he was hers first.

Mate.

"Mine," he growled as his fingers trailed down her slick hips to circle her plush ass.

Once there, he traced the perfect globes, cupping each cheek and squeezing the deliciously plump flesh there. Her ass was hot as fuck. Elissa's lust-glazed, brandy-warm stare heated under his ministrations.

Soon, the vixen's eyes flashed up at him through dark lashes like fire. Liquid heat, he thought as he touched, licked, and started to move his hips.

Inch by inch, he filled her, savoring the hiss that

escaped kiss-swollen lips. She was gorgeous like that. Sexy and hot as he buried his hard cock deep inside her.

Hunter growled, unable to stop the sound from escaping as her pussy clamped down on his cock. She felt so good.

So fucking purrfect, his Tiger seconded.

Hands on her ass, kneading the ripe flesh beneath his fingers, he lifted her and allowed her to fall back down again at her own pace, the sexy goddess filled his large hands to perfection.

But Hunter was not quite through with his exploration. He ran his greedy digits up and down her exquisite body, loving the gentle dip of her waist as it flared out to that sexy round ass. Perfect for tugging her closer.

"Hunter," she moaned his name in a husky voice that promised heaven.

"I'm ready."

Oh, fuck yes.

That was all the permission he needed. His balls tensed, dick growing harder in response. She was so hot. Sexy and earthy in a way he had never experienced with any woman, human or Shifter before. He pressed his mouth to hers, eyes open, pinning her with his gaze. He needed to watch it happen.

The first time they came together was bound to be fucking Magical. A night he'd never forget. He thrust upwards, penetrating her tight little pussy with his hard as fuck cock. She squeezed him good.

"So tight," he growled.

He tried to stay calm, to move slowly, but she was temptation itself. It was difficult when all he wanted to do was ram home and fuck her until his cum filled every inch of her womb.

Possessive much?

Yes.

Mine.

As the Neta, he was bigger and stronger than any other Tiger in his Pride. Alpha Shifters were usually in a category of their own, physically speaking. Not that he checked out other Shifters' dicks or anything. Hunter was all man. Big and thick, he needed to move carefully so as not to hurt his precious Nari. He knew this already, but what he hadn't been expecting was the fierce, primal instinct to claim her with his teeth, claws, and cum.

Like now.

It was a ferocious, urgent need, boiling in his blood. But he wanted her to enjoy this coupling as much as he did, so he would curb his enthusiasm to bite his sweet little mate.

But it was hard. She felt so fucking right. So tight and hot around his cock, if he thought about it anymore, he was going to blow.

Fuck, he growled, willing himself to slow down.

He'd allowed for her to adjust to his size before sliding in deeper and deeper, allowing more and more of his cock to slide in until he was finally buried to the hilt in her heat.

"You're so big," she moaned, clinging to his shoulders.

"Elissa," he called her name on a groan.

Focused on her, he watched as her brown eyes opened wide. Pleasure glittered in the amber deaths, some surprise too, as he filled, and filled, and filled her with his girthy length. Her channel sucked him in, clinging tightly to his shaft like velvet lined heaven.

A myriad of sensations flowed through him as she wiggled her hips, allowing her slick heat to fully encompass his cock. The first and foremost being one, single word.

Mine. Mine. MINE!

Breathing deeply, he moved.

In, out, swivel, thrust. Over and over, until his engorged dick almost slipped free of her. Elissa whimpered and clung, and he fucked and fucked and fucked. So good, so tight. Faster, harder, deeper.

Her whimper turned into something more as, with his fingers gripping her hips, he lifted, then slammed her back down onto his dick. The entire world shifted, and they both groaned in unison.

A sense of complete and perfect rightness settled over him as their pleasure built, *and built*, and built.

Fuck yes, this was right. She was right. And his. All his.

His mate was full of his cock, and it was fucking *purrfect*.

In the split second before they came together, Hunter knew he would never be the same. He held her face with one hand, angling her head where he wanted it before plundering her mouth in time with his cock.

From there on out, it was grunts and groans. No longer able to form complete sentences, he swallowed her little noises and set about drawing more from her sweet mouth.

He breathed her in. Her moans increasing with her need, excitement filled him, anticipation too. Hunter increased their rhythm. Ignoring the amount of water that sloshed over the sides of the tub. Fuck it. He could fix whatever damage they did to the flooring.

Hunter lifted his luscious mate and slammed her down again, grinding her sweet pussy onto his pubis. The slick friction of the water caused her already soft skin slide along his like silk. He fucking loved it.

Loved every bit of her. He sucked in the breathy moans that escaped her mouth as he gripped her hips and did it again. Hunter kept on repeating the movement, fucking her on his cock while her first orgasm spiraled through her tight body.

"Ohmygawd," Elissa ground out, her pussy squeezing his dick.

If possible, he grew even harder with her orgasm, and he wanted her to come again. The slide of her skin against him was that much slicker now, and with every swipe of his dick inside of her, her channel squeezed even more.

It was sexy and sensual, and he loved every minute of it. Looked forward to the many ways he would have her. But first, he was going to make her come again, this time screaming his name.

His Tiger wanted that. To feel her walls flutter around him while she lost herself in that oblivion only he could give her.

Yesssss, the animal hissed his agreement.

Chapter Twelve

Of course, that wasn't all the beast wanted. Not by a long shot. His Tiger wanted him to come too.

So fucking bad.

To fill her with his seed. To mark her with his scent from the inside out.

Grrr.

Get her swollen with his cubs.

Fuck yeah.

"Mine," he growled and nipped her earlobe, holding her there while he worked his dick inside of her, grinding her sweet pussy against him.

"Hunter," she ground out, her voice panicky.

"I've got you. Always," he replied.

Her blunt fingernails dug into his shoulders,

looking for purchase on his slippery skin. He didn't mind the pain. In fact, he rather liked it.

"You're mine, Elissa. My sweet mate, my *Nari*," he proclaimed like the Neta he was.

"Hunter?"

"Tell me you're mine," he demanded as he pumped his dick faster, harder.

He felt her pussy clench. Her channel gripping his dick in a tight hold that was bound to make him explode.

Not yet, he told himself. Not until she said what he wanted to hear.

"Elissa? Tell me!"

"Yours," she moaned, "yours, yours," she repeated, trying to move her hips.

He held her still, working hard to rein in the beast who demanded he turn her around and take her like a wild cat.

Yes, he wanted that, but he would go at his pace, not his animal's.

She mewled and whined. Her slick channel squeezing his shaft, clenching, searching for fulfillment, but he held still. Hunter knew what she wanted.

Fuck, he wanted it too.

But he needed her complete agreement first.

After this, there would be no going back.

Mine. Grrr.

"Yes, but to be mine completely, I need to mark you, Elissa," his canines slipped free, making it harder to talk.

"Need to claim you, to bite you. The whole fucking world needs to know you're mine, my mate, my *Nari*."

"Hunter, yes, please, yes," she begged.

"Thank the gods," he ground out, pressing his forehead to hers for a moment before pinning her with his stare.

"Come for me, baby, and I'll do just that. I'll make you mine, mark you with my bite," he said, his voice deep with his beast.

"Yes. Please, yes," she whimpered.

That was all he needed. Hunter altered his hold on her, dragging her hips against him. Sensations buzzed along his skin like little bolts of lightning. Elissa moaned and sighed, scratching at his shoulders, urging him on, and he did not stop.

He held her with firm hands, grinding her on his dick. Back and forth. Swirl, thrust, swirl. He kept on the torturous pace until he felt the first tremor of her orgasm squeeze his shaft.

"Hunter! Oh now, now, *now*," Elissa shouted her pleasure.

He reveled in that, in her telling the whole Pride House who it was that brought her so much pleasure. Elissa had yelled his name, and now he would claim her.

Her already tight pussy was growing incredibly tighter. Back arched, mouth open, he watched for the moment when her brown eyes glazed over with ecstasy. And there it was, one more swivel of their hips in time, and Elissa fell off that metaphorical cliff into a sea of pleasure the two of them would share for decades to come.

"Mine," he growled, wanting to claim her, her orgasm, her breathy moans, her kisses, her sighs, every last inch of her for himself.

The need to please her rode him hard. He would always want that, looked forward to finding pleasure for and with her for the rest of their lives.

Mine.

Just when he thought they couldn't climb any higher, he opened his mouth and struck. His teeth sliced through the butter soft skin between her neck and shoulder, marking her as his for all the world to see.

Her sex gripped him harder, walls convulsing on

his shaft as her orgasm sped through her trembling body. Balls tightening, dick pulsating, he couldn't wait to follow her into oblivion.

Hunter swallowed down her life's blood, searing her to his soul and his heart. The bite, triggering his own release, drew hers out longer still. He almost blacked out as immeasurable bliss soared through him.

Hunter saw stars.

No joke.

He literally saw fucking stars as his seed jetted from his cock, filling her womb, and tying them together for eternity.

The bonds of their mating securely wrapped around the two of them. Time stood still, nothing else existed, just the two of them.

Tied together forevermore as Neta to Nari. Mate to mate. Man to woman.

It was the greatest moment of his entire fucking life.

Eons later, Hunter lifted her from the tub. Her plush body was happily sated and limp. She pressed into him further, all her strength gone, and he couldn't help the satisfied grumble filling him.

He'd fucked his mate good. Just like he was supposed to. The Tiger chuffed happily contented as his luscious Nari leaned into him, trusting him to care for her. His heart swelled with pride and love.

Yes, it was too soon for that kind of declaration just yet, but all the same, he felt it to the bottom of his soul. The current of feeling was so strong, it threatened to drown him. A fucking riptide of heat, lust, caring, devotion, and more.

Shit.

He grabbed a couple of towels from the cabinet, draping one over Elissa, and carried her into the next room. Possessive and protective incતincts he'd only felt a hint of welled up quicker than the tide. She was everything to him. The first and last thing he would ever cared about for the rest of his days.

His, *no*, their bedroom was more than large enough for the two of them. Hunter hoped she liked it. The colors were a bit boring, but she could decorate it any damn way she pleased. He didn't care. As long as she was with him, he was content.

Fuck that.

Content was far too boring a word for what he felt, knowing she was with him. She belonged to him now. He'd laid his claim, and he wasn't letting go. Tiger agreed, snarling at the prospect that someone would take his sweet mate from him.

Let them try, and they will know death.

Okay, so his cat was a little fucking cranky when it came to thoughts of anyone interfering with his mating.

Mine, growled the beast.

Yes. She was his. And wasn't that fucking awesome?

Hunter laid her down gently on their big bed. Taking one of the fluffy towels from her, he proceeded to dry her off, then himself before joining her. She sighed as his skin touched hers and he relished the sound. She felt it too, the deep connection between them. It was almost tangible.

"That was amazing," she said, and snuggled into his arms.

He'd never done that before. Never held a woman after he'd had sex with her. But he wanted to now. Wanted to wrap his arms around her and hold her to him.

It was better than anything he'd ever imagined. The sweet sensation of her soft, silky skin against his, her warm breath on his chest, their mixed scent filling the air.

Sigh.

For the first time since his ascension to Neta, his Tiger felt the burden of his title lifted off his shoulders. For the first time, he was happy.

"You are amazing, my Nari. And this is only the beginning."

Desire spiked through his veins once more as she wiggled against him. The scent of her cream reached his sensitive nostrils. He ran his hands down her shoulders to her hips and ass.

Turning ever so slightly so that she was on her back, and he was hovering over her, Hunter spread her legs apart with his knees. He hissed as his hardened cock stroked along the soft skin of her thigh.

"Oh, but you couldn't possibly be ready so soon-"

"Let me tell you something else about Shifters, baby, we have an incredible healing rate."

"Hunter," she mewled his name, hips softly flexing in invitation.

She rubbed her heated body against his hardened shaft, and Hunter felt his Tiger press forward. Yes, he wanted her. Always would. With a hunger that would never, ever be fulfilled.

Her brown eyes widened as she realized just how capable he truly was, and he didn't bother to hide his grin. Elissa licked her plump lips, and he kissed them, unable to resist.

"Yes, I want you again. I will always want you, my Nari, always," he growled, pressing his lips back to hers in a soul searing kiss.

He could feel her heartbeat, taste the sweet, musk of her arousal on the air. She wanted him too.

Thank fuck, he thought.

His Tiger approved. She quivered in his embrace, a low moan rolling out of her lips as he licked his way past the valley of her breasts, over her soft belly, to her mound. Her pink sex was surrounded by neatly trimmed curls a shade darker than her long golden locks.

Hunter couldn't help himself. He pressed his face into her, inhaling her scent and drawing in her flavors.

"Need to taste you," he groaned as he placed soft, gentle kisses along her nether lips.

Gently, slowly, thanking the Fates, the universe, and whatever gods might be listening for the gift of her. He kissed her sex softly once more, then he covered her pussy with his mouth, flattening his tongue and swiping it along her slit up to her clit.

Elissa shouted. Closing her legs instinctively, but he held them open with his big hands on her thighs. He growled softly, pushing her knees wider, making room for his large shoulders.

"None of that, my gorgeous Nari. This sweet pussy is mine now," he growled.

Then he licked her again.

And again.

And again.

Back to front, and then down again. Hunter sucked and licked until he was sure she'd forgotten all her inhibitions. He held her legs wide, baring her for him. His beast not content until he kissed, licked, and tasted every slick sweet inch of her exposed flesh. Then he dove inside to taste more.

And his saucy little mate loved it. If her moaning wasn't enough to tell him, the way she grasped his head and held it in place, pushing up from her hips to ride his face, sure was.

So fucking hot.

He loved it, too. Loved the way she tasted. The way she pressed him closer until, finally, he speared her on his tongue. Her channel squeezed the muscle in response. He continued to fuck her with it, using his thumb to circle her clit until she was bucking wildly against him.

With his other hand, he circled her forbidden hole, pressing lightly until he breached the outer rim. His Tiger wanted all of her. Every fucking inch. But would she allow it?

He knew normals had sexual hang-ups Shifters barely thought about. So he went slowly. Circling and circling her tight little rosebud. Hunter fucked her pussy with his tongue and used her natural juices to lubricate the actions of his thumb.

He pushed in and out of her sweet ass slowly, softly, testing to see if she welcomed his touch.

Thank fuck, she did.

His *Nari* was a wildcat and so fucking sexy his dick was about to explode. She moaned louder, riding his face, and encouraging him to finger fuck her sweet little asshole.

All he wanted was to please her, so he kept it up. Rolling his tongue in and out of her sex, fingering her nub and her hole until she couldn't take anymore.

As her orgasm exploded, Elissa screamed his name, and he growled as her juices dribbled down his chin. But Hunter didn't stop until he'd sucked down every last drop.

Fuck, she was perfect, beautiful in the aftermath of her orgasm.

"I wanna come inside you, baby, you want that?" he asked and turned her over onto her soft belly.

Fuck, he loved how pliable she was in his arms. His mate was ready and willing for him even sated as she was now.

"Yes," she whimpered and leaned her head down, thrusting her ass into the air.

His dick pulsed with maddening need. She was so curvy, so gorgeous. He didn't understand why human men had a problem with curves. More cushion for the pushin', in his not-so-humble opinion.

"You are so fucking gorgeous, baby," he smoothed his hands over her ass and between her folds testing her readiness.

"Fuck me, Hunter. I want you to fuck me hard," she demanded.

Shit, his dick throbbed harder.

Pliable was good, demanding was better.

"Anything you want," he said and shoved his cock into her.

Her pussy sucked him in, squeezing all eleven plus inches of him, until he was buried to the hilt. Squeezing her ass in his hands, Hunter pounded into her. He wanted to go slow, really, he did, but his animal demanded he satisfy her.

Judging from the choked moans coming from Elissa's open mouth, she wanted that, too. Fuck yes, he loved knowing she wanted what he was doing to her. Loved the way she demanded him to move faster, harder.

Wasn't that just fucking gorgeous?

"Oh fuck, Hunter! Yes, more," she screamed as he continued to thrust.

His balls banged against her with each thrust, hitting her sensitive little nub. He drove deep inside her, loving her tight heat. She whimpered as he plunged his cock in and out of her slick sex, banging the headboard against the wall so hard he was sure he cracked it.

"Yes," she gasped, "there, there, there!"

He growled as he stroked that sweet spot inside of her. Loved knowing that now, he would automatically find that secret bundle of nerves each time they made love. Listening to her moans, he pumped faster, lowering his hand as he strummed her clit, adding that much more sensation. He stroked and stroked that tiny nubbin, making sure every one of her nerve endings felt what he was doing to her. On and on he moved until his sweet Elissa was screaming his name.

He pushed her farther and farther, higher and higher, until they were both panting with desperation. Dropping to all fours, he caged her in the safety of his arms while he worked his dick inside of her. Stroking her channel, he could hardly think.

His brain was full of her. Her image, her scent, her taste, the sound of her breathing.

Fuck.

When had he become a poet? He didn't know. He just knew this was right. She was right. She was everything. The only thing that mattered.

"Elissa," he growled her name around his fangs.

Shit.

He couldn't help himself he was going to mark her again. Hunter reared back just as her pussy tightened around him and struck. The sweet flavor of her life force coated his tongue, filled his mouth as his orgasm took over.

Thank fuck, she was coming too. He felt her sex grip his as they fell into ecstasy together.

Mine!

Rrrrrooooaaaaaarrrrrrrr!

Chapter Thirteen

All night long, Hunter made love to Elissa. She'd lost count of how many times he'd kissed, licked, and fucked her to orgasm.

Shivering, she came back down to earth with the stars shining overhead. During their night, it had stopped raining.

Was it only yesterday she'd been on a terrible date that had ended with her walking on the highway in the rain?

Wow. She could hardly believe it. Elissa felt like she was in a fairy tale. Maybe she was. How else could she explain lying in an enormous bed with Egyptian cotton sheets, and her Tiger mate wrapped around her?

Not to mention the delicious soreness between

her legs from the fuck marathon she'd just had with the sexy as fuck man. Elissa grinned. She had never had such mind-blowing orgasms before. Hell, that wasn't even the best part, though it was pretty fucking awesome.

The fact was Elissa Phoenix had never felt more safe, secure, wanted, and loved in her life.

Loved?

Yes, loved.

Wow. She didn't know what to think about that. Sure, love at first sight was a thing even in the human world, but she never thought she could feel that way. But now, as she lay safe and warm in her lover's arms, the word simply fit. It felt right.

Could she be in love after one night of mind-blowing sex? Well, why not? Elissa had thought herself in love before for far worse reasons.

Smiling to herself, she allowed sleep to wash over her as she snuggled into the safety of her mate's arms. Hunter growled, kissing the back of her neck in his slumber, and she sighed, happy and content for the first time in her life.

He was by far the hottest, most handsome, sexiest man she'd ever seen in her life. And he wanted her. Only her, if she were going to trust what he'd told her was the truth, and she so was. Why deny herself the chance to be happy?

She might only be a personal chef from Hoboken, but she wasn't stupid. Uncle Uzzi finding her on the side of the road and bringing her here was no accident. It was fate. Hunter really was her destiny, and Elissa was going to hold on with both hands.

Sunlight filtered through the windows and skylights, and Elissa almost forgot where she was when she woke up the next morning.

She blinked rapidly, taking in her naked state. Then she flushed as her body ached in the most delicious places.

Ooh, cramp.

She stretched carefully and waited for it to pass. It wasn't like her to get all stiff and achy. Then again it wasn't like her to have marathon sex either.

High-five self! Peace out, jealous bitches!

Hunter was a total beast. And not just because he was all stripy and furry when he Shifted into his Tiger.

The man had proven himself to be insatiable last

night. At least, where she was concerned. Oh, she'd moaned and begged, until she thought she would die of the pleasure. But still, he made her come, again and again, until she thought he'd completely broken her poor tired pussy.

Of course, he had apologized. On his knees, with his face between her thighs, and her ass hanging off the side of the bed.

Day-um.

He sure liked licking her in just about every place and position she could think of. Invented a few new ones too. Not that she'd minded. Truth be told, Elissa was a fan.

Who knew a man who looked like that would want to spend his nights eating her pussy? When he wasn't fucking her silly, that was. She didn't think she'd gotten more than a few hours of sleep, and he had even less.

Poor guy had to wake up to do something for work. He'd explained a little about his business, Maverick Development, last night. She blushed thinking about the conversation since he hadn't stopped touching her while he talked.

Hard to focus on conversation when he was thumbing her needy little clit between words. That alone had her convinced he was something not altogether human.

Speaking of his beast, Elissa wondered when she would meet his other half. He'd said soon. The Tiger wanted to make an introduction someplace open and safe, where she would not feel intimidated by his size, and she was surprisingly fine with that.

Elissa sighed and stretched, noting the pile of folded clothes at the foot of the bed. There was a sheet of paper on top. She grinned as she read the decidedly masculine scrawl.

Good morning my Nari,

I have some calls to make this morning, though I hate leaving you alone in bed. These are from my sister Jess. I had her bring them in from her store. She runs a boutique in town. She can't wait to meet you. I don't want you to worry about anything. The Pride House is yours, just take your time and relax.

I'll be back soon.

-Hunter

Okay. It wasn't exactly a love note, but still. It was something. Besides, he had to care about her. No one did the things they did to and with another person without caring for that person. Even just a little bit.

Elissa might be naïve about some things, but she

was woman enough to admit it when she caught feelings for a man. Okay, so Hunter Maverick was more than a man, but still. He'd captured her body, mind, heart, and soul.

She stretched and winced as her overworked girly bits made their tiredness known. Oh boy, was she sore! But in the most delicious way.

It wasn't all just fabulous sex, though. They'd talked and Hunter had held her all night long. He seemed just as content to simply listen to her as he was to kiss the heck out of her.

She'd never had so much attention from anyone. Certainly not from a man. Chubby blondes were considered cute in her world, but not worthy of the kind of single-minded attentiveness he'd lavished on her.

Of course, Elissa thought herself worthy. She wasn't exactly void of all self-esteem. Hence the reason she'd remained unattached for thirty years. She was not one to settle for anything.

Of course, it had seemed hopeless at times, with her inability to find even one decent man to date. But Elissa did not have to worry about that anymore. She was no longer the cute but chubby, single friend. Emphasis on single.

Elissa was taken now. She was mated to a Tiger Shifter. A big gorgeous one at that.

She giggled as she rinsed the conditioner from her hair, smiling as she wondered why he even had conditioner since his head was shaved. She noticed the pristine straight-edge razors and accessories at the end of the marble counter when she'd entered the bathroom that morning.

He must have to shave every single day to keep it so smooth and sexy. It really was a hot as fuck look. The man had one hella sexy shaped head.

Not all men could or should try to pull off a shaved head, but Hunter was beyond hot with his scalp void of hair.

Uh oh.

Her belly flopped as she went back over the hair products. Maybe he kept the expensive coconut oil conditioner for all the women he brought here?

Women he possibly had sex with. That thought brought a snarling rumble to the back of her mind, and she nearly doubled over with the strength of it. What the hell was that all about?

She frowned hard, trying to get her temper back under control. She was never one to jump to conclusions. It was better to explore the evidence than to decide based on nothing but theory.

Elissa looked back at the bottle. She didn't recall seeing it last night. She lifted it and her smile came back full force. It was full. Just like the matching coconut shampoo she'd used.

Hunter must have had his sister bring this as well. She practically bounced up and down with happiness. He'd had his sister get her some things to make her feel more at home in his big masculine room.

See, she told herself, *he was being thoughtful.*

After wrapping her freshly scrubbed body in a large bath sheet she turned to the sink to see a brand-new toothbrush, a wide tooth comb, some lotion, her brand of deodorant, and leave-in conditioner for her hair.

Wow.

She didn't know her name, but Elissa already thought Hunter's sister was awesome. She smiled and finished getting ready. When she slipped on her new clothes, she wanted to moan in pleasure.

The weather was chilly, but Elissa hated big, bulky clothing. She thoroughly approved of the stretchy blue jeans and the white cotton tank top with a simple gray cardigan to go over it.

The fabric was light and flowy without being clingy. Perfect for a bigger girl like her. She slipped on her now dry shoes and went downstairs. With her hair in a long ponytail down her back, she felt fresh and rested if not too crampy.

She'd forgone make up since she didn't have any and, truth be told, she wasn't fond of the stuff. She wasn't about to start this relationship with deception, so if he preferred her with an affinity for heavy make-up, well, he was in for some disappointment.

The thought worried her and a nagging voice in her head reminded her she should try to please her *Neta*. What the heck?

That same voice then whispered that he should remain aware that she was his Nari, and as such, was his perfect mate as is. No frills necessary.

She agreed with the sentiment, but what the actual fuck was going on inside her brain? Elissa was damn sure she had never heard voices in her whole life.

She shook her head. It must be nerves or maybe exhaustion. Last night would have tried the endurance of Olympian athletes. The thought made her smile.

Ooh yeah.

Sexy times with Hunter were definitely smile inducing. Her stomach growled and she forgot all about her wayward thoughts for the time being.

Heading for the kitchen, she thought about what she wanted to eat.

For some reason, steak sounded good. Or a big piece of fish. Odd. She didn't even like fish.

Hmm.

She stopped as she entered the room. Standing at the counter was a friendly looking younger woman with a mane of curly red hair. Something about the stranger seemed familiar to Elissa. It was in the shape of her face and the way she stood.

"Hi."

"Um, hello."

Elissa didn't feel threatened or anything. She was simply curious. The woman had been reading the back of a box of pasta and looked near to tears.

Her head shot up when Elissa shuffled forward, making herself known with the noise. She sniffed and turned familiar, teal-colored eyes to Elissa's now wide ones.

"I'm Jessica, Hunter's sister. You must be Elissa."

The woman smiled, but it didn't quite reach her eyes. She set the box of pasta down and clamped her hands in front of her. She was tall, curvy, and beautiful. But why was she upset?

"My brother told me to make you feel at home, and I wanted to have lunch ready for you, but I'm a disaster when it comes to cooking. I am so sorry," she started.

"Oh no, don't be silly," Elissa told her.

"Please, don't worry about it. It's kind of my job, cooking," she explained with a wink.

"Oh, where are my manners?! Thank you so much for the clothes and toiletries. I really appreciate it."

"I wasn't sure what you would like, so I just guessed by what you had on yesterday," Jessica replied and shrugged shyly.

Elissa noted a hint of a blush across her cheeks and her heart warmed towards her. After all, this woman was like her sister-in-law.

"Well, it fits perfectly. These jeans are the most comfortable pair I have ever worn," Elissa said, turning around to show them off.

"Really? Awesome, I try to cater to curvier girls like myself, and I am glad to hear it," Jessica replied.

She was sweet and pretty with a clean, bright complexion. Her hair was such an amazing shade of red and Elissa thought she was just beautiful.

"Wait, did you say my outfit from yesterday? I didn't meet you yesterday, did I?" Confusion clouded her eyes.

"I know. Oh geez, you must think I'm nuts!

Hunter asked me to come over and wash them for you since he didn't want any of the other males around your clothing. It's a Shifter thing," she said and scrunched up her cute nose.

"I'm so embarrassed. You didn't have to do that really," Elissa felt her blush, but relaxed all the same.

Jessica was more than friendly, and she felt no threat from the woman at all. Being new to the Shifter world, she appreciated some insider info.

"Oh, I don't mind. Besides, I am thrilled you'll be staying here."

"Do you live here too?"

"Not anymore. I live in an apartment over my store in town. But I am here a lot. This is the Pride House, so you know, there is an open-door policy to the Maverick Pride Tigers."

"Actually, I didn't know," Elissa murmured, taking in the strained silence.

"Oh, um, did I mess up? Hunter will be so mad if I make you uncomfortable. Not that he is a bully or mean in any way--- OMG! I am just messing this all up," Jessica said, and grimaced.

Elissa waited for the woman to run out of steam before replying with a patient smile.

"Look, I have a proposition for you, Jessica. How about I make our lunch, and you can fill me in on things? This way, I don't make an idiot out of myself in front of your brother or anyone else. Sound good?"

"Sure," she replied happily.

"So, you cook for a living?"

"Well, I try to. But yes, I am a chef. Graduated from a culinary institute too," Elissa smiled, and grabbed the box of pasta from her new friend's hands.

"Wow," Jessica said, her teal eyes wide.

"It's not a big deal. I just love food, as you can see," Elissa joked.

"You and me both," Jessica grinned.

"Alright, let's see what we have to work with."

Elissa began opening cabinets and removing ingredients. She almost had a heart attack as she discovered a large walk-in pantry stocked with row after row of restaurant quality ingredients.

"Oh my, this is like my dream kitchen."

Her pulse raced as she took in the wonderful assortment of goodies and gadgets before her. This only cemented her belief that fate had played her a very good hand.

Uncle Uzzi too.

Chapter Fourteen

Sparkling marble countertops, real wood cabinets, oversized terra-cotta tiles, an eight-burner stove, three sets of double wall ovens, and more.

All the appliances were state-of-the art, top quality too. Every one of them looked brand spanking new! It really was a dream kitchen.

"Well, you see, no one here really knows how to cook," Jessica explained.

"A lot of the Pride males work for Maverick Development, so they can build anything. Hunter has loads of contacts in just about every industry, so getting this stuff factory direct is like no big deal," she said.

"Really? I worked for a restaurant recently, and

the manager ordered stuff from this same manufacturer. He was told these ovens were back-ordered for a minimum of six months," Elissa replied, grinning.

"Oh, really? I could make a call and see if they can rush—"

"No, it's okay. The manager was a dick, anyway."

Elissa shrugged, and Jessica laughed.

"Well, it is not unusual for a Pride to be mostly males, with a few mates and single females scattered in between. And I'm not saying cooking is a female only thing, not at all," she was quick to insert.

"Actually, Lance, he's the youngest Tiger in Hunter's Honor Guard, that's like a group of Tigers who work directly under the Neta, anyway, he is trying to learn to cook. But he is awful, burns everything," Jessica said.

Elissa thought back to the young man who'd brought her the towel. That must be him, she thought, nodding absently while searching for just the right ingredient. She moved cans and bottles on the shelf, then paused. She couldn't help herself, she yelped.

"OMG! What is it?"

Jessica gently pushed her aside and faced the shelf of jars with her hands up like she was ready to duke it out with the pickled cauliflower. Elissa snorted.

"Are these all freshly canned?"

Row upon row of gleaming jars of canned fruit, vegetables, preserves, and pickles sat next to bundles of dried herbs. It was beautiful.

"Oh. Well, yes."

Elissa beamed at her, and the younger woman cleared her throat.

"I can't cook, but I do grow things. What we don't eat, I sort of can," Jessica said, tucking her hair behind her ears.

The woman blushed bright pink, and Elissa reached out and hugged her. She had nothing but love for someone who could grow and pickle veggies. Back in her apartment, she had a small herb garden on the fire escape, but the thought of having a vegetable patch was just amazing.

"Is the garden here? Can I help? OMG! I am so excited, tell me more," Elissa said and pulled a few jars of peeled plum tomatoes off the shelf.

With her grandmother's recipe for her Sunday meat sauce simmering on the stove, Elissa instructed Jessica to fill a huge pot with water and salt before setting it to boil.

"Wow, that much salt?"

"Oh yeah. Then you don't need any extra when you sauce it," she explained.

Elissa figured four pounds of pasta should be enough if Jessica was telling the truth about Shifter appetites. Judging from Hunter's insatiable lust the previous night, she tended towards believing the pretty redhead. On second thought, she turned and grabbed two more boxes of the 100% pure semolina pasta.

After mixing up the ingredients for meatballs in a giant stainless-steel bowl, Elissa taught Jessica how to scoop and mold them properly. After a while they had roughly six dozen ready for the oven on cookie sheets. Once the ovens reached the correct temperature, in they went.

"This really is some kitchen," Elissa sighed, and set the timer.

"Wow. I can't believe we did all this already," Jessica replied, looking at all the food they'd prepared.

"Wait till you see how I cook for the holidays," Elissa said, only half joking.

"OMG! I can't wait. Hunter is going to love this. He's been looking for a cook for a long time, and the interior designer who worked with him on the renovations thought she was the woman for the job. I have never seen my brother shut down a woman like that, and fast. He never was one to mess around, though he's had plenty of girlfriends. Oh no, I, I didn't mean-" she stuttered when Elissa's face fell.

"It's okay, Jessica, I mean, of course he's had experience. I mean, just look at him," Elissa replied and tried to shrug it off.

The sting of unshed tears had her blinking, and she turned away. Sheesh! Why was she so emotional? She turned back to the fridge to dig out some grated cheese.

"No seriously, Lissa. Hunter hasn't dated anyone in years. He's been waiting for his mate all this time. He's been waiting for *you*," Jessica said in earnest.

Elissa nodded. She wanted to believe her, but it was difficult. How could she compare to a Shifter female? Looking at Jessica's tall frame and pretty face, Elissa figured she was up against some serious competition when it came to the women he was used to.

"I see what you're doing, Lissa," she said and shook her head.

"Don't go there. Look, I opened my big mouth when I shouldn't have, but I swear on my mother's grave, a mated Shifter never ever cheats on his mate. Like never ever. He couldn't, even if he wanted to.

The animal inside of him wouldn't allow it. Besides, if my brother ever thought about it, I'd kick his ass for you!"

"Okay," Elissa said, laughing now. "I believe you. It's just new to me."

"I understand, and I apologize again. You have no idea how relieved we all are that he found you. You see, the whole Pride needs you."

"What do you mean?"

"Well, someone's been starting a rumor that he wasn't fit to lead because he did not have a mate."

"What? Is Hunter in danger?"

"Huh? No! He's the strongest one out of all of us. His leadership wasn't even challenged or anything, just empty rumors from some faceless guy who cited some old Pride laws about needing a mate to rule," Jessica said.

She shrugged again, but Elissa's stomach clenched. Was that why Hunter had contacted Uncle Uzzi? She'd thought he wanted a mate for himself, but if this was true, then it was possible he had ulterior motives.

His position as Neta was being threatened by someone who was too cowardly for an outright challenge. That was truly a terrible thing, but it made her wonder.

Was yesterday real? Was that his actual response to *her* or to his circumstances? Maybe he faked it to keep her by him, and, therefore, keep his position safe? Last night had been the most poignant night of her life, but what if it was all just a lie?

The sounds of heavy footsteps coming towards her made Elissa jump. She frowned as a group of enormous, slightly sweaty men came trudging through the door. Each was a giant to her, and one stood a full head above the rest. They looked tired and worn, a layer of dust covering most of them. Not that it took away from their attractiveness. She had to admit, they were a great looking group of guys.

"What is that awesome smell?" one asked.

"Don't tell me Jess learned to cook overnight or something?" added another.

Elissa was standing off to the side, unnoticed so far, but she watched as one young man stepped closer to the pot of sauce. It was the guy from last night, the one who'd handed Hunter the towel. She figured he was Lance.

Waiting for his reaction, she watched him as he sniffed the pot of sauce and moaned, but not before getting a whack to the back of his head from Jessica.

Good for you, thought Elissa.

"Sheesh! Have some manners in front of your Nari," snarled Jessica.

Elissa was too pleased to see all the men sniffing the air and rubbing their stomachs, to be offended by anyone's behavior.

"Sorry, Nari," Lance said, rubbing his head.

The men stilled and turned, staring at her. Gulp. She heard more than one growl and panicked for a moment. Were six pounds of pasta going to be enough? They looked like they could eat twice that.

"Everyone, your Nari is making lunch."

"She is?"

"Yeah, so you better go wash up, and make sure you leave your work stuff in the mudroom!" Jessica hissed at the men.

She flicked more than one hand that tried to creep towards the rack of cooling yeast rolls with a kitchen towel. The men whined and grunted, but they did as she said, each one bowing slightly to Elissa before running down the hall.

The largest male tipped his head in a polite bow as he walked by, and she gulped and took a step back. He was gigantic, and he moved differently than the rest of the men, who reminded her of a group of alley cats she once saw working together to take down a garbage can.

They mumbled as they walked by her, using the same word Jess had used. It was what Hunter had called her the night before, *Nari*. She'd thought it meant mate, but that couldn't be right if they were all saying that to her.

She just had no idea what it really meant, so she simply stood still, smiling, and nodding at them in turn. The tallest one paused for a brief moment and looked at her with intense brown eyes that bled to black before lowering his head in a deep sort of bow. He whispered something that barely made out. It sounded suspiciously like a vow.

"On my honor, I swear my allegiance and vow to protect you, *Nari*," the large male nodded once more.

He ignored Jessica when the woman was looking, only to glance behind him the second she turned her attention elsewhere. The tall man stared for a long moment before walking away to the section of the Pride House that held single rooms.

"Lance! You forgot your boots again," Jessica called, ignoring the big man.

She didn't seem to even see him as she growled and ran after Lance. If the younger Tiger was what Elissa suspected, then the guy was something of a player.

Definitely not looking to settle down with a mate

forever and ever, which was what she'd picked up from her new sister-in-law. Did the saucy redhead have a thing for the baby-faced Tiger? Elissa hoped not. That kind of unrequited love or lust could be a real bummer.

Hmm.

She just hoped Jessica didn't get hurt. For the time being, she had her own mating to think about. It almost made her giggle, but she stopped herself once the hair on the back of her neck stood up.

Elissa felt the atmosphere change. In that same instant, she knew she was being watched. Inhaling a calming breath, she startled, almost sure she'd tasted anger and a perverse sort of pleasure in the air. But that wasn't possible, was it?

Shaking it off, she pressed a hand to her abdomen as a cramp hit her so hard, she almost gasped aloud. Biting her tongue, she turned to find one man standing silently in the kitchen.

A tremor of fear slid down her spine as she recognized the male. He smirked and entered the room slowly. The male stood with his hands on his hips, insolently raking her with his hard gaze, tipping his head as he sucked in a long, deep breath.

It was more than just a look this time. He was positively glowering at her. It was Blake, the Pride

PURRFECTLY MATED

Beta. Elissa was not a fan of the creep who'd tried so hard to intimidate Uncle Uzzi and herself just the night before.

She kept her breathing even and turned her back on him. Bullies were only effective when given attention. She'd learned that lesson long ago. Unless ignored, they held all the cards.

So, instead of dwelling on the man who obviously hated her for whatever reason, she chose to tend the food. Cooking was always her safe place. Where she went to escape. She donned a pair of oven mitts and checked on the several baking dishes she'd filled with pasta, ricotta, fresh basil, tomato sauce, and a dash of grated pecorino romano cheese, topped with a drizzle of olive oil.

The meatballs were almost finished, as was the huge tray of chicken thighs and legs topped with panko breadcrumbs and slices of garlic and lemon. She also had a platter of roasted veggies she'd added on a whim.

Thank goodness, too. The guys who'd just run through the kitchen looked huge and hungry.

"You know, I wouldn't make myself at home if I were you," Blake said, suddenly right behind her.

The creep had slunk across the kitchen without making a single noise. Elissa gritted her teeth, refusing to retreat. Instead, back straight, she turned her head and met his glowering gaze with a single raised eyebrow.

"Yeah? Why is that?"

"Hunter knows better than to let some human stand in the way of what's best for the Pride. He might fuck you for a while, but that's all you'll be. Just some whore he keeps to swallow his cum," he spat.

Elissa was proud of herself for not blinking. That was the vilest thing anyone had ever said to her. Blake was a fucking pig, not a Tiger, and she was not going to sink to his level.

"I might be a human, but I believe it is the Neta who decides what is best for the Pride. That's not you, is it, Blake?"

Elissa tossed that little bit of snark back at the now growling male. She knew she'd hit the nail on the head when his eyes glowed with his Tiger. Did Hunter see what she did when she looked at his so-called Beta?

She needed to tell her mate. Protective feelings rose inside her, and she was practically trembling in outrage. The bastard was after his position, whether or not Hunter realized it.

Blake was staring at her with an angry, crazed

expression on his face. With a mockery of a smile plastered to his mug, he took another menacing step towards her. Elissa swallowed hard, wondering if she should call for help.

"Nari?" inquired a rumbling voice from behind her. "You need a hand in here?"

She exhaled, grateful for the interruption and turned with a wide smile on her face. She was determined not to show Blake how afraid she'd been.

"We're fine---" Blake began, but she cut him off.

Asshole.

"Actually, I need a hand. These trays are heavier than I thought. Would you help me bring them to the table?"

"Of course, Nari. How about you Blake? You gonna help?"

The tall Shifter's voice dropped to a low growl, and she wondered if this was one of those posturing things she'd seen on *Animal World*.

The shorter man growled and walked past them both, slapping his work gloves roughly in his palm as he left the room. With any luck, he'd leave the house too, she thought.

Elissa closed her eyes and swallowed, relief flowing through her. Shit. She had that cramp again and pressed her hand to her stomach until it went away. She almost forgot she wasn't alone when the large man cleared his throat.

"If I may be so bold," he said, waiting for her nod to continue. "If anyone bothers you when Hunter isn't around, Nari, you just let me know. I'm not a Tiger, and maybe I was raised different, but us Bears know better than to growl at a female, and a mated one at that."

"Thank you, uh, I don't know your name," Elissa replied, feeling more relieved by the second.

"My name is Brayden Smith," he nodded, but didn't move to take her hand.

More Shifter customs, she supposed.

"Nice to meet you, Brayden. You can call me Elissa. Did you say *Bear*?"

"Yes, Elissa," he grinned. "I am a Black Bear Shifter, but Hunter still took me in when I left my Clan. He isn't prejudiced or a hard ass like some other Shifters."

"I see," She said, appreciating the glimpse into her mate's past.

"Blake is the Pride Beta," Brayden further explained.

"And he should know better than to snarl at you. Oh, and the reason I'm not taking your hand is because I'm not suicidal.," he said with a wide grin.

"When your mate gets here, he's gonna want to be sure you carry his scent alone. Blake already got too close to you. I imagine Hunter will take him to task for that. I know, I sure as hell would," Brayden finished.

He nodded, and she felt her nerves loosen under his kind gaze. The male seemed friendly and polite. Definitely more respectful than Blake had been.

"Thank you, Brayden," she said.

Elissa meant it, too. She was truly grateful for his intrusion on what was a very uncomfortable meeting with the Pride Beta.

"Oh, uh, I think those meatballs are ready."

"Oh! Yes, you're right. There you go," she handed him a set of oven mitts and pointed to the right oven.

While she worked to get the other trays of food sorted, the other men came in one at a time to carry food and introduce themselves.

They each carried more than she could have, and the trays of food were waiting on the table when she walked into the dining room. Jessica sat with her eyes on her plate, and she wondered what had upset her friend. She noted Lance had not come down to eat and cast a sympathetic glance at the pretty redhead.

C.D. GORRI

"Oh, uh, Lance had a date," Jessica explained, nodding at the empty chair.

Elissa smiled. He was a kid. It wasn't unusual for them to date and blow off meals with family, *er*, Pride, was it?

"Nari? I mean *Elissa*, please allow me to introduce Tyler, Mikey, Reg, and Pierce. The five of us work under Blake. He's the foreman for the state road crew," Brayden said, interrupting the awkward silence.

She stared at the five huge men and swallowed. These guys had muscles on their muscles, each one handsome as sin. Though no one came close to Hunter.

He was in a class all by himself. Just thinking about him did things to her insides she couldn't possibly explain and didn't want to name. Did it make her a total slut that she was drooling over the guy she'd only just met?

Maybe.

But whatever. She knew her mind, trusted herself, and she wanted him. The end. Period. Nobody's business but her own.

Mine, that new voice in her head spoke up, and she felt warm to her toes.

Chapter Fifteen

Hunter had explained a bit about his business last night. Maverick Development was a small but well-known construction company that specialized in demolition. Shifter strength and all that.

He'd also explained he was trying to renew contracts the company had with the federal, state, and municipal governments for years. Everything was happening at once, and he was busier than usual.

After speaking with Jess, Elissa saw a connection. It seemed the rumors about his inability to run the Pride were hurting his business as well. She frowned heavily at the thought.

There was so much about Hunter and the Pride

that she didn't know, but she was determined to be an asset. Yes, he was practically a stranger, but she didn't believe for a minute he was incapable of handling business. He certainly handled theirs.

Me-ow.

She snickered coughed to cover up the suddenly naughty turn of her thoughts. But who could blame her? Hunter Maverick was a veritable god in bed.

Or the bathtub.

So lost in her thoughts, Elissa hardly heard the laughter and noise around her. It was nice, though. The natural comradery around her was not faked, forced, or feigned in any way.

She felt comfortable around them.

All of them.

These strange men. Her new sister, Jessica. Hunter. Most of all, Hunter.

They were all the Pride, her Pride now. Something inside her told her she was safe, and she felt relaxed with them as if she'd known them all for years.

"If I eat all the meatballs, you think Hunter will freak out on me?" Tyler asked.

"Nah, he's got a mate now to make him more," Mikey answered.

"Shut up, Neanderthal! Women don't just sit

around chained to the kitchen all day waiting for their big bad mates to get home!" Jessica snarled.

"It's okay, actually I love cooking---"

Elissa tried to break it up, but they were having too much fun tossing out crude names.

"Don't get your tail in a twist, *Jessi-cat*," Reg snickered, earning him a glare from Brayden.

"Children! Stop it right now or no dessert," Elissa scolded in her best authoritative voice.

Almost immediately, the group of Shifters went quiet, with a few murmured apologies here and there.

"Can I, uh, that is, what did you make for dessert?" Reg asked.

Everyone giggled, and a roll might have gotten tossed at Reg. Mikey snagged it out of the air before it made contact and put the whole thing in his mouth. These guys could really pack it away!

She wondered at the reason she felt so comfortable with them, in response, that voice in the back of her mind reminded her once more it was her job.

You are their Nari. Let them see your wisdom.

She stood up quickly, ignoring the strange voice and the quivering in the pit of her stomach. It really was a good time for dessert.

She went to the kitchen to retrieve the pies she'd

made using the canned sweet cherries Jessica had put up the previous season mixed with some pitted tart cherries she'd found in the walk-in freezer. A little sugar, a bit of lemon zest, a healthy splash of rum and, *voila*, her special cherries jubilee pies.

Elissa had figured they'd appreciate some nice homemade pies after their meal. Especially served with her special freshly whipped vanilla cream. Besides, she'd needed something to do with her hands while everything else was cooking in the oven.

They'd turned out wonderfully. Perfectly browned and glistening with sugar crystals. She took a deep sniff, noting with some shock the detailed assortment of delicate flavors she'd been able to catalog with each breath.

Holy cow. That was new.

She was always proud of her work when it was deserving, but she'd never felt quite so in tune with the ingredients before. Perhaps it was the high quality of the foods and their organic nature. She couldn't say for sure, and the rumble in her head seemed to disagree with that assessment.

Elissa ignored the feeling that something else was going on with her, choosing to focus on the present. She walked over to the baker's racks and retrieved the tray of pies from where they sat, cooling after they'd finished baking.

The soft shuffle of feet behind her made her tense. Enraged at the intrusion, she stilled with the pies in her hand and tried to get a handle on her sudden rage. Her spine was tingling like mad. The voice inside of her mind growling like a beast.

It was more than a sixth sense. It was as if a whole new person had suddenly sprung to life inside of her. The thought was vaguely terrifying, but she had no time to dwell on that. There was something, er, someone headed her way. Whoever it was, the person would be there soon.

He's here, that strange voice hissed excitedly.

Elissa turned around slowly. Joy and happiness welled up inside as she took him in.

Hunter's home.

His brilliant, teal eyes glittered at her from across the kitchen. Heat filled her belly and moistened her sex as her pulse raced in anticipation.

Her hands suddenly felt heavy, but before she could drop the pies right on the floor, there he was, standing in front of her. Her mate took the heavy tray from her hands and placed it on the counter.

Her heart thundered in her chest as he moved in closer, pinning her to the counter with his body. She licked her lips. Desire blossomed deep inside of her. It begged to be let out.

"Mate," he breathed the word.

"Yes," she returned.

The warm, minty air from his parted lips caressed her neck as he breathed in her scent and she closed her eyes, just breathing him in. His thick, long-fingered hands found her nape and tugged on her ponytail until her hair was free to spill down her back and across her shoulders in a mass of blonde curls.

Hunter took her face in his hands, and she reopened her eyes, meeting his gold-rimmed gaze. He tilted her head back, pressing soft lips across her jaw and chin until finally treating her mouth to the same wonderful teasing.

His big, thick hands dropped, touching her everywhere with care and reverence. He caressed her waist, his fingers tracing the underside of her breasts while their tongues danced together.

She felt so good, so in tune with their kiss. It was passionate beyond comparison. A celebration of their reunion, even after such a short parting. Elissa sighed and leaned on him, trusting him to hold her up with their embrace.

She wondered if every parting would end up

with this kind of meeting between them, and she trembled.

I hope so.

Heaven, the man could kiss! Her toes were curling from the somewhat chaste contact. Her stomach warmed, nipples pebbled, and panties grew wet as his chest brushed against hers. She couldn't remain idle, not if she wanted to stay sane.

Reaching up with shaky hands, she traced the line of his jaw up to his dark eyebrows, loving the way they furrowed as if he were kissing the most precious thing in the world to him. Could she be that? He was to her. And more. So much more.

He continued to press his lips to hers, slowly moving back and forth until she was desperate for him. She followed his lead, parting her mouth on a groan, and that was when he plundered.

When she opened her eyes, she saw his Tiger still sparkling in his gaze. Gold-rimmed the teal irises bore into hers. He looked regal and otherworldly.

Heat pooled in her belly, moistening her sex as she responded to him. She was turning into a nympho for the man. Never before had she been so attuned to another person, but with Hunter, she could practically feel his desire, and it fueled her own.

Her hands raked down his back until she was cupping his firm ass, squeezing it for all she was worth. She wanted him. Now. Here. Was ready to beg until a cough sounded from close by.

"Oh, damn! Guys, this is the kitchen. I mean, yuck, gross! Hunter, I expect this from you, but Lissa, really? You're just gonna grab his ass like that in here? Where we prepare *the food* we eat? OMG, ugh, I just threw up in my mouth a little," Jessica screeched.

Hunter whipped his head around, a snarl on his face, and Elissa nearly laughed out loud when he finally realized it was his sister in the kitchen with them. The younger woman covered her eyes with one hand as she felt around on the counter for her keys.

Elissa giggled, and Hunter raised his eyebrow at her before dropping a kiss on her forehead and sighing.

"Jess, I see you met Elissa," Hunter began.

"Yeah. And can I say, she is great! Seriously! Totally love her, bro. Now, I would stay for some dessert to celebrate with you, but I need to go home and bleach my eyeballs."

"Bleach your eyeballs?" Elissa asked.

"Yeah. Duh. You were groping my big brother's

butt, and that was like three on my top five things of stuff I never want to see. *Like never ever.*"

"Alright, Jess, that's enough," Hunter said, but Elissa could tell he was amused.

"Bye, Jess. Call me later," Elissa said.

"Yeah, not later, *and this is so gross for me to say*, but I imagine you will be busy. But I will talk to you tomorrow. Bye-bye," she waved, and left the room with a dramatic full body shiver.

Wise ass, Elissa thought, but she liked the woman. Liked her even more when Hunter laughed at her antics. Elissa wrapped her arms around him from behind, loving the rumble of his chest as he watched his sister break out of there like a bat out of hell.

"Sorry about that, baby. I got carried away," he said as he led her inside the dining room.

"That's alright. I missed you too," she replied, suddenly feeling shy in front of him.

"Neta," Brayden stood up and tilted his head, bearing his throat to Hunter. He waited for her mate to sit down before joining him at the table.

"I have some things to discuss with you, but I, uh, understand if you need to wait until tomorrow," the Bear Shifter said.

He was blushing a bright pink, kind of endearing really. As was his refusal to make eye contact with his leader. Elissa's brow furrowed until it finally dawned on her what he meant.

The big Bear figured she and Hunter were about to engage in a marathon boinkfest. Not that she was opposed to the idea, but she understood her mate's position with a clarity that was almost scary.

Hunter needed to take care of the Pride, and as his Nari, she felt the same need. Smiling at them, Elissa stood up and indicated the table laden with food.

"Hunter, why don't you eat while I get some coffee on to go with the pies I made? I'll bring them out in a few. Oh, do you like coffee or tea?" she asked, a little embarrassed that she didn't know which he preferred.

"You sure, baby?" Hunter asked. "I can help you---"

"Of course, I'm sure," she answered before getting a tally of what the others wanted to drink with dessert.

"Brayden? Coffee or tea?" she asked the Bear last.

"Oh, uh, thank you ma'am. Coffee will be fine."

"What did I say about that ma'am business?"

"Sorry, Elissa," he lowered his head some more, and tilted it even further to the side.

Jessica had explained behavior like that to her.

Brayden was bearing his neck to his leader. A sign of trust, respect, and most of all submission to Hunter's position and dominance.

It would also serve to stop the Bear from inadvertently insulting his *Neta* by addressing his mate so informally. Now, even though Jessica had explained things like that to her earlier, but there was nothing like seeing it up close and personal.

She had so much to learn, but Elissa was more than up for the task. She grabbed her cell phone from the table and slipped it into her pocket before returning to the quiet kitchen. She'd just started a large pot of coffee brewing, then dialed her roommate.

"Oh my God! Elissa, is that you?"

"Yes, Gretchen, it's me."

"I am so sorry! My phone died last night, and I didn't see your messages until after I did Mrs. Little's hair this morning. I was just beside myself! I had no idea the guy was a creep!"

"It's okay. I met someone, well, an older guy kind of gave me a lift after your would be Romeo left me stranded-"

"Oh my God! You hitchhiked? You could have died!"

"No, it's okay, Gretchen. Look, he was a sweet old

guy and he introduced me to another guy, and well, we kind of hit it off," Elissa said evasively.

"Wait. What? You total slut."

Elissa could practically hear Gretchen's grin across the line.

"So, did you sleep with him? Was he any good?"

"Gretchen! I am not going to tell you that, but I think you might have to find a new roommate," she whispered.

"Wait. Are you serious? Elissa! How am I gonna make the rent," she wailed.

"Don't worry. I will come up with a plan. In the meantime, I want you to come visit me. Soon, okay?"

"Aren't you coming home for Thanksgiving?"

"I think I'll be spending it here. I want you to come too."

"Okay, I'll try to after the holiday rush. You know all my clients need their hair done before they see family. Seriously though, are you alright? Like really alright?"

"Yes, I am. I know it seems crazy, but I'm happy. Now, promise me you will come for Thanksgiving, okay?"

"Lissa, I don't know if I can afford it---"

"No worries. I'll send a car to get you."

"A car? Elissa, just who are you shacked up with? A prince or something?"

"Something like that," she smiled.

"I'll talk to you later."

Still grinning, she dug through the cabinets for a nice wood tray. Elissa loaded it with fixings for coffee and several plates for the sliced pie.

It was all so homey. She loved it. Elissa was already settling in, and she could not be happier. She loved to cook for large groups. Homemade meals that regular folks were too busy with life to have the time to make. It was like her dream job.

And Hunter was her dream man. Butterflies knocked around inside her stomach while she carried the tray inside. She almost missed a step when she saw Brayden had gone and was replaced with someone she had not counted on seeing just then.

Blake.

Something inside of her hissed and spat at the man's intrusion. She agreed with that new and rumbly voice inside her head. It wanted him gone, just as she did. With everything inside of her.

She'd deal with her sudden case of multiple personalities in a second, right then, she had to show strength for her mate. Straightening her spine, Elissa didn't even flinch when Blake jumped up to take the tray from her.

The male's claws were extended, and he managed to scratch her hand. What the heck? For some unfathomable reason, he'd had his Tiger's claws unsheathed.

Even more outstanding, he hadn't been able to cut through her skin. Looking down, she gasped in surprise, which was nothing compared to the shock in his angry glare.

"Baby, you alright?"

Hunter looked up from his plate of pasta, which she'd noted with some pride, was almost empty.

"I'm fine. Blake's hands are just cold."

"He shouldn't have touched you," Hunter snarled.

He turned on the weaker man and Blake immediately averted his gaze, bearing his throat. Something inside of her was immediately placated by the show of jealousy and temper.

"Apologies, *Neta*," Blake mumbled.

Insincere apologies meant nothing to Elissa, and she knew he did not mean it. She glared as he turned and set the tray he'd taken from her down on the table.

His greasy smile made her want to dry heave, but she waited to see what the Beta would say by means of explanation. Going to Hunter's side, she sat in the empty chair he pulled out for her while

Blake searched for a suitable reason for touching her.

"I simply meant to assist you, *Nari*," he said, lying easily.

She'd already asked the other males of the Pride to call her by her first name, but not him. Something about Blake made her skin crawl, and she did not want him calling her at all. It made her question if she was doing the right thing, jumping into a world she knew so little about. But however she felt about Blake, her love for Hunter was even more potent.

"Take care, Blake. Anyone who even appears to harm my Nari will have me to deal with," Hunter's warning was spoken in a low whisper not meant for her ears.

She realized this, and yet she had heard him.
Odd.

Odder still was the way he'd turned to her with a smile, as if she hadn't just heard him threaten the man who was supposed to be his most trusted male. Maybe he didn't know she'd heard him. So much to talk about but being near him made her keenly aware that she'd much rather be alone with him than here. They could talk later.

"Thank you for lunch and this unexpected treat. It looks wonderful, my love."

Hunter smiled at her, and suddenly, her mood lifted. Any doubts caused by the Beta were instantly replaced by the sheer strength of her affection for him. The knowledge that this man, *her mate*, would protect her was overwhelming.

Good male.

Good mate

Mine.

Mine, repeated that strange growly voice inside of her.

Then Elissa closed her eyes as a wave of pain so powerful, it threatened to topple her crashed over her body like waves against the shore.

Grrrr.

Chapter Sixteen

After a grueling day dealing with a bunch of bureaucratic assholes, Hunter could not wait to get home.

All day long, his inner beast had been pacing. Pissed off and missing his mate, his Tiger had threatened to make more than one appearance in the office. Finally, upon arriving home to find his sexy mate in the kitchen, Hunter had felt a pang of need so forceful, he had no choice but to give in.

He'd expected to find her sulking or angry that he'd been gone so long. It hadn't been his intention to stay away, but the entire Pride depended on his ability to take care of them. They needed these contracts, but the Shifters he usually dealt with, ones who'd inserted themselves among the normals, had heard the rumors. They were reluctant to sign papers when they did not believe he could hold on to his Pride.

When he found the motherfucker responsible, Hunter was going to tear the guy's head off. But back to Elissa. She hadn't been pouting or complaining as other past girlfriends had when he needed to work.

In fact, she'd been busy caring for the Pride, and that made his beast want to roar his pleasure. Hell, he'd almost devoured her on the spot. Were it not for Jess and her untimely interruption, he might have done just that.

So sweet and tempting, so sexy and fierce, Elissa was proving herself more than capable to run the Pride right beside him. That was something he never dared even dream. To find a mate who was a true Nari, capable of ruling at his side. And a human to boot! His Tiger chuffed and growled appreciatively.

Grrrrrrr.

When they retreated to the dining room, he found some of his Pride waiting for him.

"Neta," Brayden spoke in that respectful way the Bear Shifter had about him.

It was one reason Hunter liked the man so much. Brayden was a good man and Bear. He'd survived the unthinkable and had joined them after leaving his Clan.

It was a terrible thing, losing one's mate. Hunter did not know the details of the Bear's history, only that he'd almost gone rogue after nearly being driven mad by the loss. Suddenly, he understood and shuddered at the thought. Having just found Elissa, Hunter couldn't fathom not having her in his life.

Even after only one day, she had managed to change everything. Her natural warmth and energy had him turning to her like a flower searching out the sunlight. She was like that.

His sun. His moon. His entire world.

"Here," she'd said in her sexy little voice, and he'd obeyed.

Sitting down as she handed him a plate. Hunter took the heavy dish from her hands and began filling it with the wonderful meal she had prepared.

He gave himself a heaping serving of pasta, meatballs, chicken, and veggies and soft, fluffy rolls that appeared freshly baked.

"You made all this?"

"Do you like it?" she countered.

"Like it?" he scoffed, and took her hand, kissing the palm.

He moaned at the heavenly scents that assaulted

him. So many delicious flavors to try, but none as sweet as her. He tugged her closer and stole a kiss, just to thank her once more, but dammit, he never wanted to stop.

He loved the way she opened for him, kissing him with intense heat before shyly ending their kiss with a pointed glance at Brayden.

Fucking Bear.

Hunter had forgotten about him.

She'd offered to get the pie and make some coffee, and he thanked her. Smiling so broadly, his face hurt as he watched her move about the dining room. He did not like the way she hefted the large tray back into the kitchen, and one glance had Reg running to take it from her.

The other males stood, clearing the table as they left. Hunter made a mental note to remind every Pride House resident and guest to clean up after themselves. His mate was no one's maid.

He would also hire on more household staff. Someone to task with things like cleaning and carrying the heavy stuff so his Nari could be free to do what she loved and not be burdened by the mess.

Elissa might love to cook, but she was by no means required to do so. She was the Nari and would be treated as such. Even more amazing than his increasingly possessive and protective feelings for her after so short a time, was Hunter somehow knew that something inside her already recognized her role.

He'd watched how she'd stood up and managed to set the Bear at ease while placating her mate's hunger for food. A true matriarch for their Pride.

"So, Brayden, what can I do for you?"

"Neta, thank you for talking with me."

"Of course," he waved away the formality of Brayden's response and dug in.

Damn.

The woman could cook. He might have mated her based on the things she could do to a dish of pasta alone.

"Good, isn't it? Reg damn near got down on his knees and proposed after he tried a meatball."

The Bear grinned, and Hunter growled.

Fucking Bear.

"Mine," he said.

"Yes, *Neta*," the Bear said, and stopped grinning.

"I need to talk to you about a couple of things. The foremost being, I think something needs to be done about Blake."

"Blake? You may want to rephrase that, Brayden. Blake is the Beta."

"And we both know better," said the Bear.

"There is something not right with Blake, Neta. I think you know that."

It was then that the true dominance of the Bear Shifter before him revealed itself. Hunter grunted, staring at the Bear for a full second before the other animal lowered his gaze.

Satisfied with the show of submission and respect, Hunter released a chuff. His Tiger had taken in the Bear when he'd been alone in the world. He recognized him as an ally.

"What are you saying exactly, Brayden? Are you declaring you would like to challenge Blake formally for the position of Beta?"

"I don't think I have a choice," Brayden replied with a heavy sigh.

"Why do you say that?"

"Because I saw him with the Nari---"

"What did you say?" Hunter spoke carefully, easing back from the table.

He looked down at his empty plate. Since when did he inhale food like that?

Since it was fucking edible, answered his beast.

He couldn't remember the last time he tasted such an exquisite meal. But that was not the issue right then. He needed to understand exactly what

Brayden was saying.

"I couldn't hear what he was saying too clearly, but the Nari was not happy with whatever it was. Also, Blake was close to her, Neta, too close. He should have treated her with more respect---"

Brayden stopped, his inner Bear pushing forward as Hunter's growl built and built until it reverberated in the room. A tiger in the wild had the ability to paralyze his prey with a low frequency infrasound that rendered its prey frozen still.

A Tiger Shifter, specifically an Alpha, could sometimes emit such a sound. Specifically, when his or her mate was threatened. Right then, Hunter's Tiger was really pissed off.

The beast demanded the blood of any and all who threatened his precious mate, even for a second. If Brayden was telling the truth, and everything said he was, Hunter was going to have no choice but to throw down with his second.

"Get me Blake," he commanded.

Brayden rose without saying a word and left the room to do his bidding. He appreciated the man wanting to challenge his Beta, but if Blake was out of line with his mate, that would be for him alone to rectify.

Five minutes later, Blake strolled into the room.

The fucker was pretty damn arrogant to be walking in like he'd done nothing wrong, but Hunter would play his game.

For now.

"Hunter, I mean, Neta," he said, and casually bared his throat as he took his seat to Hunter's left.

"Speak," Hunter commanded.

Blake shrugged, looking everywhere but at Hunter. He seemed agitated, but still, he did not challenge him directly. Hunter would have to wait for satisfaction.

"What?"

"I said go on, explain yourself."

"What? Your bitch Bear running his mouth off?"

Blake snarled and shook his head. Sweat dotted his forehead and Hunter's Tiger chuffed angrily.

"Dammit, Hunter, he doesn't belong here anymore than she does! She's a human. A fucking chubby normal, for fuck's sake. She can't be the Nari."

"Watch your fucking mouth, Blake!"

"What? You can't seriously think she will bear the future of this Pride! I mean, you fucked her, fine. Chase all the chubby chicks you want. Hell, even I can see why you'd go for that, but that doesn't make a mating---"

Hunter let his rolling growl press deeper into the male, using a bit of his power as the most dominant of the Pride to press down on him. This fucker needed reminding why Hunter was in charge.

"Listen to me, Blake. You are here at *my* leisure and as long as you can be of use to the Pride. Elissa Phoenix is my fated mate. She is the Maverick pride Nari, which makes her far more important than you or anyone else. Now, I will slaughter anyone who threatens her or our mating without a second thought. Do you understand me?"

"Hunter, all due respect, the laws say you must be *truly mated*, that can only mean to another Shifter-"

"She is *mine*," Hunter snarled.

He allowed a little more power to seep into his voice. The weight of it must have been grueling because Blake practically fell out of the chair. His beast was barely placated when Blake finally did slink down to his knees under the force of his Neta's displeasure.

Hunter sniffed the air, licking his lips. He scented hostility, anger, and deceit. Wasn't that something? Maybe Brayden would have his challenge after all. If Hunter allowed Blake to live that long.

He turned to the slimy male, meeting the crafty smile on his Beta's lips before loosening his hold on him through his powers as Neta. The door separating the kitchen from the dining room swung open, revealing Elissa.

She looked good enough to eat in her tight jeans and white tank top. A sweater was tied around her hips, and he smiled, thinking she must have gotten warm while she cooked.

He noted the way her smile faltered when she saw Blake and not Brayden by his side. Something was definitely going on. Blake practically leapt from his position on the floor to take the tray from her. Hunter used the moment to try to get a grip on his emotions.

His mate was everything good and beautiful in the world. He could not wait to really start their lives together, and he didn't need Blake causing any disruptions.

Just imagining the way Elissa would be with their cubs made his skin itch to find out. But she would need time, but could he help it if he was impatient?

She'd probably let them crawl all over her. He grinned at the thought. So lost in his own musings he'd not been prepared for her little yelp of pain. Snarling, he jumped out of his seat when he heard it to see his Beta standing far too fucking close.

Her eyes flashed to his. Hunter thought he saw

fear there for a second, but it passed so quickly, he pushed the thought aside. Elissa's gasp had sent him to her side, and Blake backed up.

Good thing too. Hunter's beast was outraged. Had he scented her blood, Blake would have died before he took his next breath.

As it was, the Beta walked away with the tray and set down the coffee, cream, plates, and slices of pie on the table nonchalantly. Hunter's Tiger urged him to grab his Beta by his scruff and pin him down for upsetting Elissa at all.

At the same time he wanted to take her upstairs, so he could taste her most secret, sweetest pie again and again. The cherry pie on the table smelled heavenly, but it was nothing compared to the one between his mate's legs.

That thought brought on a ton of possessive snarling and growling inside his head. Shit. He was a mess.

Mine, growled the animal.

Hunter shook his head and watched Elissa standing before his Beta with strength and determination in her gaze until it turned to him. Then it changed. Power still wrapped around her like a protective blanket, but there was something more. Her usually dark brown eyes glittered at him, turning to gold right before she moaned aloud and doubled over in pain.

"Elissa!"

Hunter roared, catching her before she could collapse to the hard floor. She tensed in his arms and opened her mouth.

Fucking hell!

A set of long fangs protruded from her mouth, long and sharp. Next was a wave of pain and as it rolled through her, it nearly sent him to his knees.

The matebond, he thought as he gritted his teeth against a second, sharp stabbing pain. He was connected to her through their bond and feeling what she was.

Puspa.

The word popped into his head, and panic gripped him for a second. No wonder she was growling. His poor, beautiful mate was in the throes of something that was the stuff of legends.

The Puspa had started, and it was happening *now*. Like really happening.

His mate was going through something profound and extraordinary. Something that would leave the two of them vulnerable, and with Blake in the room. Not very fucking likely.

Hunter tore from the space, anxious to get his

mate away from the threat of another male while she underwent the painful process that was Puspa.

With Elissa on his arms, he retreated to the larger, open living room. Throwing back his head, he roared a warning to everyone in the Pride House.

His mating bite had awakened something inside of her. Something wondrous and exceedingly rare. Something this fucker was not going to take from him.

Inside the large living room, Hunter spotted Brayden and Reg lounging on the sofa, waiting for him to finish his meeting, he assumed.

"Neta?" Brayden questioned.

The Bear stood and looked at Elissa's prone form with raised eyebrows.

"It's the Puspa," he growled. "Call Mikey at the clinic and tell him what I said."

Hunter placed Elissa gently on the sofa. Behind him, he felt his enemy, Blake, stalking him. When had this happened?

When had their friendship gone bad? Fuck. He heard the snap of bones, the tearing of muscles, as the man changed forms from human to beast.

"It is not right, Hunter. She should not be the Nari. You leave me no choice," Blake grunted.

He was barely coherent beneath his fangs. Fur

sprouted across his chest, more tawny than orange, and he became his animal with each breath.

"Elissa is the Nari, and you are no longer of the Maverick Pride. I banish you," Hunter snarled.

His change was completely different from Blake's painful process. Highly attuned to his beast, one moment was all it took for Hunter to go from skin to his own fur. Just one thought, and he was his animal.

As the Pride Neta, he was the strongest of the males, but that was not all. Hunter was also the largest.

His Tiger erupted from him, a bright orange and black beast twice the size of a normal Bengal Tiger. He stood in front of his Nari and roared to his entire Pride.

Those in their human forms understood he was in charge here. This was his domain. And Blake was his to kill.

He had no idea the man had gotten so twisted, but as the pieces fell into place, he saw he'd been blind to it the entire time.

It was you undermining me this whole time! He hurled the thought at Blake in his Tiger form.

I was right to do so. You are weak. An abomination. Taking a human as mate is weakness.

Hunter snarled. He had been aware that someone was undermining him, but he would never have looked at Blake as the culprit. Coming to terms with the fact his college friend was his secret enemy was going to be tough. Blake had been close to going rogue when they'd met. Hunter had felt for the lone Tiger. He had allowed his sympathies to bring him into the fold. He'd always assumed giving him a home and Pride would ensure the man's loyalty.

Hell. How much of their so-called friendship had been faked and forced? How many memories, stories, and jokes told were all but lies? And now, the fucker thought to endanger his Nari?

Hell no.

Fury filled the Neta's veins. Blake's smaller Tiger hissed and spat as the rest of the men pushed the furniture out of the way, careful with Elissa. The two big cats circled each other, but his focus was split between the enemy and his mate.

Elissa's whimpers and moans, not to mention the pain he felt through their bond, were calling his attention away. But even a momentary lapse could cost him his life, And worse, hers.

Hunter would not allow that. He would never let this sonovabitch to put his mate in harm's way. And no, he didn't trust the fucker to fight honorably. He snarled and chuffed, calling to the males in his Honor Guard to stand watch.

They would all bear witness to the battle about to enfold. One question plagued him. Why had Hunter ever trusted this male? He could only blame his youthful ideals on the gross misjudgment, but this was not the time to ponder the question.

Blake was fighting dirty. The smaller, yet deadly Tiger Shifter, scratched at him with lethal claws, ripping a long gash open on his back leg. Hunter felt the sting of his wounds and roared in fury.

The bastard was looking to distract Hunter while he tried to lunge forward to sink his teeth into his exposed neck. Hunter anticipated it and drove him back with a hard shove from his Tiger's immense body.

The male was too close to his mate for Hunter's comfort. He snarled and growled, grabbing Blake with his claws, he shoved him aside and raked the wicked sharp, six-inch long claws down both sides. Blood poured from the wounds, but Hunter's animal was not satisfied.

His beast snarled as he scented his enemy's blood in the air. He'd given Blake two gory gouges, one on each side. Again, he swiped at Blake's animal, sinking his front claws deeper through the other male's thick fur. He sliced through skin and muscle, all the way down to the bone. And yet, Hunter's beast still wanted more.

Fuck that.

He demanded more from the male. Blood and sweat dripped down their furry bodies as they crashed into oner another. Blake's hateful comments and prejudice against Elissa drove Hunter's fury to new heights.

His Tiger was enraged by the weaker male's actions. The attack, too, without the right of challenge, was a coward's way. How dare the male try to endanger what belonged to Hunter?

His mate.

His Pride.

His business.

For those offenses, the asshole should already be dead. They wrestled and fought until Hunter gained the upper hands. He clamped his teeth around the smaller Tiger's neck, ready to shake him like a rag doll, when a soft whimper brought his head up.

Elissa, his Tiger chuffed her name.

Hunter's mate needed him. He couldn't dally with this filth anymore, so he spat him out, using his enormous paws to swat the male into a nearby wall.

Blake lay unconscious and Hunter turned towards Elissa.

His Nari was suffering. The scent of her pain and fear had him racing through his change. Hunter ignored the blood coating his skin and knelt at her side, barking orders for his men to lock the bastard up in the old barn.

The Pride had a cell they used to house rogues or enemies until judgement could be made. Hunter obeyed the laws of their kind, and he would be looking forward to a legal challenge to the death when the time was right. Until then, the piece of shit would answer to the Council of Shifters for his actions.

Hunter would abide by their ruling. But right then, he didn't give a fuck. It didn't matter what anyone else said or did.

Only Elissa mattered.

Mine.

Chapter Seventeen

Fire coursed through Elissa's veins. Something was happening. Something strange and a little bit scary. She was in the middle of a wrestling match, but it was internal.

A strange male tried to touch her forehead. She hissed, wanting to bite and claw at him. Only the fact she vaguely recognized what he was trying to do stopped her from scratching the man's eyes out.

Elissa did not know the man well enough to have an opinion of him, but her reasoning was simple. She simply didn't want his hands on her. She only wanted Hunter.

He was the only male allowed to touch her. Ever. In any way, shape, or form.

Mine, hissed that strange voice she'd been hearing all day.

She barely had time to register it before more agony assaulted her senses. Elissa always had a high tolerance for pain, but this was unlike anything she'd ever experienced.

It was like something was trying to claw its way out of her. Literally.

In the periphery of her vision, she saw Hunter kneeling next to her. He was naked and covered in blood. Several scratches covered his skin, but they seemed to be healing already. Something Shifters could apparently do and with ease.

Thank fuck.

Kind of cool, really. She wondered if he could help with whatever was happening to her. She clenched her teeth as another wave of cramping and nausea hit her hard.

Dammit.

She wanted to scream, but couldn't unlock her jaw to let out a sound. Vaguely, as if from underwater, she heard him shouting to his men. He wanted them to get Blake out of there, to lock him up.

Good, Elissa thought.

But another part of her, a darker, more animalistic part, roared at the idea. A raspy voice spoke inside her mind, and she went still with shock.

Bastard. We should hunt him for daring to touch.

Um, what the fuck? Who is that talking in my head?

Elissa shook all over. Was she losing her mind? Was the last twenty-four hours some sort of hallucination and had she finally gone crazy?

No, you have not lost your mind. I am you. You are me. We are one. Let me show you.

What had first felt like an alien invasion suddenly made complete sense as a pure white Bengal Tiger took shape in Elissa's mind's eye.

Ohmyfuckinggod!

Pain squeezed at her gut, but instead of fighting it like she had been doing, Elissa exhaled and embraced it. Finally, she understood what was happening to her.

Yes. That is it. It is the Puspa, little one. We are blossoming into something new. Together we will be a strong Nari for our mate.

Yes. Blossoming.

Elissa agreed. She liked that imagery. She completely relaxed her muscles. Her breathing evened out, and her pulse steadied.

She heard Hunter in the periphery of her mind. He was panicking. Her mate pressed his head against her chest, trying to listen for her heartbeat. From one soft breath to the next she felt a ripple of Magic sweep over her body.

Her suddenly four times the size as normal body.

She blinked rapidly, turning on her stomach so that she could stand on all fours. She shook her head. All fours?

EEEEEEEEEK!

The entire world seemed slightly askew. The soft leather of the sofa tore under her sharp claws, and the sound of chortles and whispers around her made her snarl. She chuffed a warning, hating that she'd made such a mess. Leaping off the couch onto the floor, she turned and scented the air.

Finally, she found Hunter still kneeling beside her. A wide grin spread across his gorgeous face, and she padded over to him. Sitting on her hindquarters, Elissa bumped him gently with her head.

"Nari, my sweet Elissa, you are so gorgeous in your fur," his chest rumbled with his beast, and this version of her found she liked that idea very much.

She bumped him in the shoulder and stood up, hoping he would catch on. Elissa turned her back on her mate, swatting her tail at him. Her animal would not have done so with anyone else. She trusted him though.

Always.

Elissa chuffed again and moved towards the large sliding door in the back of the destroyed living room. She growled at the two men, who stood like dummies just staring at her. She had to admit she enjoyed their reaction once they caught on. They bowed their heads, dropping their gazes immediately, and opened the doors.

It was only right they do so, her animal reminded her. Pride members should never look at her directly. She was their Nari. The strongest female in the Pride. They would do well to remember that. The males stepped aside, allowing her to pass through the door unobstructed.

Good, she thought, *he can live.*

Her human side frowned at her cat.

Tiger! Not a cat, hissed the animal in her brain.

Whatever, her human half said. *No killing any of the Pride.*

Hmpff, said her beast.

Her tail swayed from side to side, and furry Elissa turned around to catch her mate still staring. She opened her mouth wide, showing him the glint of her teeth.

The urge to run, to be chased by him, was overpowering everything else. She growled once, catching his stare.

Now.

After giving Hunter one long, hard look before vaulting outside, Elissa took off into the wet stretch of forest behind the Pride House. A loud roar sounded from behind her, and she knew it was him.

Hunter.

Her beast practically purred in excitement. She pushed harder, running faster, using her newfound senses to take her through what looked like a well-trodden path.

Her nose told her Hunter stalked this trail often. She chuffed again happily. She wanted to be close to him in every way and leading him on a chase that would most assuredly end with them, mating under the setting sun seemed fine to her.

It had only been twenty-four hours, and Elissa had been through and seen more changes than she'd ever thought possible. And yet, all she felt was happiness radiating through her. After all, what wasn't there to like?

She'd found out Shifters were real. Had mated one. And now she was one.

Holy crap!

If that wasn't a happily ever after, she didn't

know what was. The sound of wet leaves scrunching behind her told her she wasn't alone any longer.

Looking to her left, she saw the regal beast of her mate gazing at her. His gold-rimmed teal colored gaze glowed as he stared at her. Hunter licked his long fangs, and she shivered in anticipation.

Wanting to touch him, she stepped forward, human feet replacing her paws in an instant. It was cold outside, but she didn't seem to feel it.

"Hunter," she said and released a heavy sigh.

"You are so beautiful."

Elissa reached forward and brushed her hands over the thick fur of his neck and head. His Tiger rumbled approvingly. She continued with her tactile perusal of him, loving the warmth and his rumbling sounds.

Soon though, his fur receded, and she was touching hot skin. Hunter's arms wrapped tightly around her, and Elissa smiled at the feel of him.

"Mate," he growled against her neck, his voice thick with his beast.

"Lemme take you home, Nari, get you warm," he said.

"Oh yeah, I'm kinda naked out here," she said, looking down kinda shocked to discover she was completely bare.

"Clothes don't survive the change, I'm afraid, but I could have Jess bring you more of the same if you liked them?"

His concern touched her.

"Thank you, I would like that, but what about everyone else? I don't want everyone to stare at me," she bit her lip.

She knew from Jess that Shifters had no qualms about being nude in front of each other, but this was all so new to her. As if he hadn't considered that, he scooped her up in his arms and turned to the house, but not before loosing a loud roar that seemed to echo off the land.

The rumbling continued long after he'd closed his mouth, and it thrilled her to her bones. Hunter turned to her chest heaving and kissed her hard on the mouth. One word was all he said before he ran back through the woods.

"Mine!"

Her Tiger purred affectionately. She'd recognized her mate's warning to the others. Any members of the Pride lurking around the house better make themselves scarce, or she pitied what would happen to them.

In less than three minutes, Hunter had them both safe and warm under the warm spray of his incredible six-head shower in the master bathroom. It was luxurious and decadent, and just fucking incredible.

Elissa really, really liked this room. She clung to him under the water as he shampooed and soaped her body from top to bottom. She hissed her pleasure as he ran his callused fingers over the hardened pebbles that were her nipples.

Carefully, he cupped her breasts and rinsed the suds from them, treating the rest of her body to more of the same. Carefully, thoroughly, he washed and rinsed, treating her to the utmost care.

By the time he knelt down, she was panting with need. She wanted his mouth on her, his tongue stroking her, but big beast that he was, he teased her first instead.

"Oh, I will get you back," she promised, mouth open on a sigh as his lips nuzzled her nether regions.

Hunter ran his hands up her hips to her rounded ass and back down to her thighs. All the while he nibbled and kissed, light feathery touches that made her want more. He nudged her legs apart with his hands, using one massive shoulder to support one as he lifted her foot, encouraging her to rest her thigh on him.

"Hunter," she moaned, holding onto his head while he licked at her slick folds.

His chest rumbled, the vibrations spreading through his mouth, all the way down her body as he latched onto her pussy in a fierce, all-consuming kiss.

"Mate," she moaned.

Next, he speared her on his tongue. The dominant move satisfying both the woman and the Tiger that lived inside of her.

Whatever happened, whatever was going to happen, all she knew was it felt too good not to be right. Too fast for real life? Not hers. No way in hell.

Elissa might be new to having a furry and fangy side, but as long as he was with her, she was more than fine with it.

Hell.

She could face anything as long as she had him.

Yes, replied her Tiger. All she could think while he laved attention on her was that she wanted this, him, everything he had to offer. And in turn, she wanted to give him everything she had.

Together, we are purrfect, her Tiger pressed the thought into her head.

Yes, she agreed. *And more. I want more. I want everything.*

As if sensing her thoughts, he gripped her hips with his hand and moved his tongue faster. Stroking her from ass to clit, he licked and sucked, plundering and owning her entire body.

She felt the familiar tightening of her belly and knew she was about to come, and she reveled in it. Elissa couldn't wait to ride that effervescent wave with her mate.

My Mate.

My Neta.

All Mine.

Faster and faster he moved, using that spectacularly talented tongue of his until Elissa's back arched and she felt the first tingles of ecstasy flow through her. Hunter must have felt her impending bliss, cause the big sexy bastard flattened his tongue along her clit, and then he purred.

Prrrrrrrr.

"Hunter!" Elissa cried his name as she came, and came, and came, knowing she was safe and free in her mate's arms to let go completely and ride the pleasure he'd given her.

She was still in its grip, when sexy beast that he was, Hunter had her up and over and was filling her from behind, stuffing her so full of his big thick cock she didn't know where she ended, and he began.

Just as it should be.

Chapter Eighteen

Hunter didn't know what he did to deserve such a sexy as fuck mate, but he wasn't about to question it. Not when worshipping her with his body was so much more fun.

He felt her pussy convulse around his tongue, and he worked harder. Sucking, licking, scraping his fang along her little bundle of nerves, and finally, flattening his tongue against her clit and purring until the sexy little she-Cat was screaming his name.

He could've enjoyed that position for quite some time, but his mate was pulling on his head until he came up, grinning.

"Mine," he growled, and swept her off her feet.

Before her orgasm could completely cease, he

flipped her over, settling her hands on the tile, and plunged into her welcoming heat from behind. Her ripe ass was perfect for cushioning his thrusts as he fucked her harder and faster than ever before.

Sure, they had explored each other, but she was a Shifter now. His sweet Elissa could take more, and he didn't have to hold back. Her walls clenched tight around his erection, a second orgasm building strength as he fucked her hard against the wall of the shower.

"Fuck, baby, you feel so good. So tight, so hot. I love you so fucking much, my Nari, my mate," he growled love and naughty words into her ear.

The cold tiles under her palms held her up as he pounded into her. Later he would make love to her slowly and thoroughly like she deserved, but right now, with his Tiger riding him hard, Hunter needed this.

He needed fast and hard. An acclimation of their mating, of her Puspa, of the strengthening and sealing of their matebond.

"Elissa," he hissed.

"Gonna come, Hunter. Make me come," she growled.

"Yes. Anything, mate. Come with me," he commanded.

His beast would accept nothing less than her complete submission to his demand. And his Elissa seemed to know that. She was ready and willing, and wasn't that fucking incredible?

"Yes, yes, yes!"

One, two, three more hard thrusts, and that was all it took. Hunter ground his dick into her, clutching her waist tightly in his hands, then he felt her shudder and he was right there with her.

His cock spurted his seed deep inside, coating his mate's womb, marking her with his scent. Hunter felt his fangs elongate, and couldn't help himself, he bit her right over her left shoulder, placing another mating mark on her smooth skin.

Fuck, he thought, going cross eyed with pleasure. His bite made her pussy squeeze him even tighter, milking every drop of cum from him.

"Mine!"

He roared, and the sound echoed off the shower walls. Several minutes later, after he'd towel dried both himself and his boneless and exhausted mate. Hunter held her, cradling her to him, in their warm, dry bed.

"Hunter?"

"Hmm?"

"What is going to happen to Blake?"

His animal tensed with the question. The beast was angry he hadn't gone for the kill, but he understood tending to his mate was much more important than the insignificant male.

"He will be locked in a cell until the Council convenes to try him."

"Are we safe? From him I mean?"

"Elissa," he said, his voice thick with his animal.

"You are protected. Always. I would die to keep you safe."

"I know, Hunter," she replied, sighing his name.

"Can I ask another question?"

Her sweet voice was tired, but so full of contentment he could've died a happy man right then. He squeezed her against Him, kissing her forehead.

No, chuffed his beast.

The animal did not want to think about dying when he had a beautiful mate to take care of and impregnate with his cubs.

"Of course. What is it, my Nari?"

"Are you going to explain what happened to me?"

Once more, his anxiety rose. What if she was upset over the fact she was no longer human? Would she reject what had happened? Or worse, would she reject him?

He had no choice but to answer. His sweet mate deserved the truth from his lips.

"Our people call it Puspa," Hunter began.

"Puspa, yes, I heard you say it before, but I thought never happened anymore," she said shyly.

"No need for that now, my beautiful Nari. The Puspa is very rare, as is your white Tiger. You are a gift, my love. Unique, beautiful, and beyond comparison. The fact you were able to communicate to the animal with words that early is amazing. Some Shifters only ever get impressions and feelings from their beasts."

"What do you mean?"

Elissa sat up and gazed at him with hauntingly beautiful brown eyes. Circled in thick, dark lashes, she blinked slowly. Hunter cleared his throat. He wanted her so badly, but he knew she needed this time to talk with him. To understand everything that had just happened to her.

"You are my Nari. A born leader. Alpha fem to all the Pride, and you are a white Bengal Tiger, sweet Elissa. That alone is very rare. Not to mention, you are also my *fated mate*. The Fates who decreed you mine also gifted you, us really, with the Puspa. It means *blossoming*. That is when a normal, *or human*, is taken as a mate and the union awakens what has always been inside of you."

"So are you saying I was always a Shifter?"

"Not necessarily, though stranger things have happened, my love. Who knows how many people have latent Shifter genes? I mean, we've been here since the beginning too, so it isn't all that farfetched."

"I see," she said, though he felt her confusion.

"You can ask me anything, my love, I will do my best to answer," concern clouded his voice.

He wanted, no, *he needed*, her to trust him and to be as happy with their mating as he was.

"I guess I just wondered why the rest of the world doesn't know about Shifters?"

"Oh, well, people see what they want to, my love," he murmured and pressed his lips to her hair.

His Tiger settled, knowing that it was her curiosity that had her confused and not the state of her feelings.

"Hunter?"

"Yes, baby?"

The endearments fell from his tongue easily. Something that had never happened to him before, but he couldn't help it.

"Is it too soon to tell you I think I love you?"

Her chin dug into his chest as she turned to look

at him, the words slipping from her plump lips. Hunter's heart squeezed in his chest, but he couldn't speak. Not yet.

Fuck.

He was acting like a pussy. What was next? Was he going to tear up during diaper commercials and shit?

Grow up, the Tiger hissed, *you love her. As you should. She is ours. Now tell her.*

"Considering how much I love you, no, I don't think it's too soon."

He turned, so that he was covering her with his body. Loving the way she opened up to receive him, Hunter leaned down and nuzzled her lips, kissing her with all the feelings he could not express with words.

The warm vanilla sugar flavor that was all her burst along his tongue as he tangled with hers. Needing some relief from the ever-present desire he felt for his mate, Hunter ran his erect shaft along the seam of her lips.

"I'm sorry I'm not good with words, but I swear to the gods, the Fates, the whole universe, I will love you with every inch of my being until I blink out of any and all existences, my love."

"I love you so much," she replied and mashed her mouth to his.

His cock nudged her slit, and the wetness there told him he was not alone in his need. She purred beneath him, and that was when he damn near lost his mind. The vibrations flowing through her to him made the teasing little strokes of his dick along her sex that much better.

"Shit, baby, gonna blow if you don't stop that," he growled at her.

She nipped his lip in response.

"Sorry," she whispered, but her eyes said she wasn't.

Elissa flexed her hips against his cock while lapping at the small drop of blood that welled up from where her fang had scraped the sensitive flesh. And if that wasn't hot as fuck, he didn't know what was.

But she didn't stop there. His sweet as sugar, and apparently aggressive as hell mate, used her newly found Shifter strength to flip him over and reversed their positions.

"Fuck, Elissa," he growled as she sat astride him.

Her blonde hair cascaded down her shoulder in a wave of gold as she raised her arms and lifted her hips. Claw tipped fingers gripping her hips, he tried to be gentle as she slid up and down his shaft.

She allowed his dick to pop free then found the tip with her sex, kissing it with her wet pussy lips before sliding back down and grinding into him. Every withdrawal and slide pushed his system into overdrive. He could barely hang on as she rode him good and hard.

"Hunter, so good, love," she growled, and her brown eyes glowed gold as her pace increased.

"Take what you need, mate."

"You. Need you."

"That's it. Ride me, baby, anything you want," he said and truly he meant it.

"Mine," she said.

Elissa scored her nails down his chest, the added bite of pain made his balls tighten, his cock eager to spew his seed deep inside her womb.

There was nothing as sexy as seeing his curvaceous, gorgeous mate riding him. Her eyes were glazed with lust, mouth open as she swerved her hips, grinding her pretty pussy on his cock.

She increased the pace, her channel twitching all around his shaft. It was fucking glorious. He felt every inch of her as she slid and swiveled, massaging him with her walls. Together they panted, and

Hunter sat up. He teased her nipples with his tongue, finally sucking one into his mouth and tugging with his teeth.

The added bite seemed to give her more of what she needed. Hands gripping her hips, he forced her to move faster and harder on his dick. Her moans grew and so did the pressure building inside of him.

He thrust upwards, furiously pumping from beneath her sumptuous body. His dick ached with the need to come. But he needed her to reach the pinnacle before he did.

"! Come for me, mate," he growled, releasing her with one hand so he could thumb her sweet little clit.

One hard stroke had her moaning, back arching as she clung to his shoulders. The slapping sound of their bodies fucking was sweet music to his ears. He never wanted to stop, but he knew it was inevitable.

His mate bared her teeth, fangs elongated in her mouth. He saw her Tiger in her eyes and for once the Neta of the Maverick Pride bared his throat, succumbing to his mate's bite with fierce pleasure he'd never savored before. As she sucked on the wound, his cock throbbed and pulsed within her tight heat.

Their *matebond* pulsed with new strength. Hunter

himself was a fiery ball of need and lust for his mate. *And more.* So much more.

Possession, pride, caring, desire, heat, and love, *yes love*, burned throughout his entire body and both sides of his soul too. She was his now.

Forevermore.

Elissa moaned as she swallowed down his essence, her body convulsed around him. The force of her orgasm had him exploding inside of her. Hunter roared thunderously as he came. His claws pierced her hips, marking her again as his and his alone.

It slammed into him with all the force of a supernova. Momentarily blinded by the power of it, he moved on instinct, mashing his lips to hers.

Gasping for air, they kissed and nuzzled and held each other through all the shivers and moans in the aftermath of their furious yet gentle lovemaking.

"Love you," she sighed.

"I love you, my Nari," he whispered and kissed her lips. She purred softly and he nuzzled her neck, savoring the sweet warm smell of her.

She smelled like home. Her Tiger's essence mixing her warm vanilla sugar scent with that of the Pride. He supposed that was just how things should be. She was his home now that they were mated.

Yes, the Tiger agreed.

Purrfectly mated.

He gave her one more kiss before he allowed exhaustion to claim them both. He wanted her again already, but that could wait. They had forever to be with each other.

Chapter Nineteen

Elissa stirred the large pot of chicken soup and smiled to herself. It was still raining out, and she figured soup would do everyone some good.

The weather at Maverick Point was a lot harsher than her hometown. Must have something to do with the altitude. The mountain loomed beyond the picture window, and she smiled. Autumn was notoriously unpredictable in the Garden State, but the leaves were gorgeous this time of year.

Late November could see days in the low seventies and nights in the teens. It was totally crazy. Of course, now that she was a Shifter, she ran a little hotter. But still, all the rain and wind made for chilly weather fur or not.

Elissa sighed, taking in the small changes she'd already made to the Pride House. She'd officially moved all her things in from her Hoboken apartment.

Her chubby Italian chef statue with the "specials" chalkboard sat on a place of esteem on the marble counter. Hunter said she could do anything she wanted in the kitchen, it was hers now, so she'd decided on transforming it a bit.

Yellow and white checked curtains matched the potholders and dish towels she'd had tucked away from her grandmother. They made the clinically clean kitchen appear homey in her eyes, and the others seemed pleased too. Of course, she always had fresh baked goods and something savory cooking on the stove or in one of the ovens. For the record, Tigers ate a shit ton.

It was the type of space she'd always dreamed of having. Of course, seeing Gretchen and explaining her whirlwind romance without really explaining it had been difficult.

With Hunter's insistence, she'd paid the next month's rent directly to the building superintendent since she knew her friend would not appreciate the handout. That should give the woman time to find a new roommate or a better, less costly place to move.

Maverick Point was certainly nice, Elissa thought with a grin.

Before she'd left, Elissa had bullied Gretchen into promising to come by for Thanksgiving. Her Tiger purred at the thought. It would be good to see her friend again in Elissa's new home.

She'd been worried about her place in the Pride, but they'd settled into a nice routine. Her love of cooking had been readily welcomed by the lot of them. The inner circle who lived in the Pride House especially appreciated her abilities.

One thing she'd learned quickly was that Shifters sure could eat! Their appetites were enormous. Keeping up with just those who lived there was like running a restaurant.

She hadn't wanted to find a job outside the Pride, but Elissa was not someone who could handle being idle. It was kind of awesome, being able to cook and create menus for people who enjoyed home cooked meals. Besides, Hunter had frowned hard when she mentioned working and he explained the thought of her being away from him for any serious length of time sent his Tiger down a possessive spiral.

Seeing as how she felt the same, she was fine with that. Elissa craved the man all the time. At first, it shocked her he seemed to want her back just as much. His wildly possessive streak was also surprising and flattering. Some might say unhealthy, but they weren't Shifters.

Hunter hated it when other people got too close to her. Something she found endearing, which surprised the shit out of her. She'd never been much for the jealous type, but now that she had her own possessive as hell, she-cat lurking inside, she understood his position.

Her silly kitty liked her mate possessive. In fact, it was one hell of a turn on. The Tiger even agreed that she should not leave their den to work. Especially, since her mate had even gone so far as to ground himself.

Instead of overseeing the many jobs Maverick Development had going on, Hunter had worked out of his home office as often as he could. Today, he had urgent business that took him out of the house, but she understood. Besides, she had Tigers to feed. It pleased her inner beast to know there would be a terrific meal waiting when he got back.

"It's because you're newly mated. His Tiger needs the contact, yours too. It's cute, and yet completely creepy."

Jessica had explained it after that first few days when they hardly left their room. The younger Tiger was constantly reminding everyone she was creeped out by her brother getting it on with anyone.

Still, even then Elissa didn't quite understand, she appreciated it. It was a level of devotion and affection she had not expected. How could she when she'd never experienced or witnessed anything like it?

As far as Elissa was concerned, she was the luckiest damn woman alive. So, what if her new furry self came with extra hairy legs? She simply adjusted from shaving every third day to every other day.

Easy as pie.

A smile haunted her lips as she remembered the way her mate had kissed her that morning from her toe to her, well, *to her lips* when she'd complained about it.

Sigh.

Moan.

Sigh again.

"Baby, you can shave, don't shave, whatever you want. I don't care, as long as you know this here, and all that luscious cream you got inside, is all mine. My pretty pussy."

Prrrrrrrr.

Hunter had growled and licked her until she begged him to make her come. After that, she totally believed him when he said he didn't give a fuck about when she wanted to shave.

Her big kitty didn't care about his mate's hairy legs as long as he got his cream.

Check.

Elissa was one lucky beyotch. She hummed as she chopped up some flat parsley and tossed it into the steaming pot. Today was the first day Hunter had left her alone to check out a new crew. She'd humored him while he'd hemmed and hawed over leaving her until, finally, she'd pushed his ass out the front door.

"I could stay and have Brayden do it," he'd growled.

"Hunter, stop being a pussy. I'll be fine, go on," she'd insisted.

Elissa couldn't blame him, really. He was upset that the Council hadn't come by yet to pick up Blake for his trial. Elissa frowned about that, too. She was sure he'd told Reg to find out what the delay was the day before yesterday. But then they got distracted playing a game of *hide the Tiger tail* and she forgot to follow up.

Oh well.

She was sure Reg followed his Neta's word without question. Forty-eight hours to get a handle on the elusive Council was probably normal. Right?

She checked the clock just as thunder erupted outside. Shit. More rain. Jessica was due to arrive any minute for their lunch date. Well, at least she'd picked a good menu.

Chicken soup coupled with thick sopressata and tomato sandwiches on fresh baked Italian bread. Oh, and caramel fudge brownies for dessert.

Yum.

Elissa didn't know why, but she'd woken up ravenous that morning. More than usual. She heard the front door open and waited for her friend as she pulled down two large soup bowls.

Hmm. She supposed Jess was her sister-in-law and her friend, right? Whatever. It didn't matter. She was just so happy today.

"Jess, is that you? I'm just finishing up the soup," she turned with the ladle in her hand.

Shock made her drop the utensil, but she didn't scream.

"What are you doing in here?" Elissa asked in a calm voice which surprised the shit out of her given the man who'd tried to kill her mate, and her, was standing in front of her.

Blake was dripping from the sudden rain. His clothes dripped all over the polished floors, and that angered Elissa.

"What am *I* doing here? You stupid slut. I belong here! It's you who has no place here," Blake snarled, swiping his hand across the distance between them.

She jumped back, knocking the bowls onto the floor with a loud crash. Elissa gasped as his claws made contact despite her efforts, scratching her wrist. Blake laughed crazily and pulled her to him. His rancid breath in her face made her want to hurl.

"Let go of me," she demanded.

"Or what, bitch? Without Hunter here to protect you, how do you figure you'll get away? You are all alone, *Nari*," he said, snarling that last word.

Blake raised his hand, hitting her across her face. Pain exploded in her cheek, but she turned and scratched him back, trying to get out of his grip just as Jessica came running in.

"She's not alone," Jessica yelled.

The redhead ran into the room, her claws extended, but she wasn't fast enough. Blake sidestepped her and smacked Jess across the face, pushing her in the process. The force of the hit had Jessica slamming into the far cabinet and slumping to the floor in an unconscious heap. That really pissed Elissa's Tiger off.

"You shouldn't have done that," she growled, her eyes burning with the force of her Tiger.

She could see the moment he realized he'd fucked up. It was in the panicked flare of his nostrils. The acrid stench of his fear mixed in with a touch of madness burned her sensitive nose.

"How? You're just a normal," Blake spat at her and backed up.

Elissa recalled Hunter had knocked his sorry ass out before the Puspa had been finished with her.

Too fucking bad for him.

It was not her job to make sure he was informed about her new inner Tiger. In fact, she felt a mild hint of satisfaction when he looked shocked. The weaker male dropped her arm as if it burned him.

"No. That is where you are wrong, Blake. I am not just anything. I am the Nari of the Maverick Pride, and what you are doing is treason," she growled with the force of her animal urging her forward.

Weakened and confused, Blake backed up. He slipped on the puddle that had formed beneath him, landing on his back before her. Elissa saw the opening and pounced.

Straddling his chest with her weight, she held his arms beneath her knees and used one claw-tipped hand to squeeze his throat. Blake bucked, but she was immovable.

"Lissa?" Jessica's slurred words had her focusing on her friend. Fortunately, the younger female was not seriously injured. Unfortunately, Blake used her distraction as an opening to hit Elissa in the head, sending her across the room.

Her head ached, especially around her ear where Blake had struck her. Fucking coward. She felt dizzy and nauseous.

Shit.

Her hand went to her stomach, but she forced herself to drop the telling move. She'd only just found out and had yet to tell her mate. Worry made her careless and Blake scrambled to his feet and grabbed her by the hair, slamming her into the kitchen island.

"Dammit," she snarled, whipping around it.

She moved faster than ever before, facing him in a crouched stance she'd seen MMA fighters on television use. She wasn't even sure she knew how to fight, but her Tiger was there to urge her into action, and the beast did.

"Ha, did you think you could beat me? You're nothing but a whore!"

"How did you get out, Blake? Was it Reg? Did he let you out?"

The wheels had started turning, and the man was

the only one of them who'd had contact with Blake the past few days. It hurt to think one of the Pride, one of Hunter's Honor Guard, could have strayed, but she had to ask.

"That little prick turned his back on me the second Hunter claimed you. I had to convince him to help me this time. They all forgot me, and after everything we did together! I had them all eating out of my hand, citing the old laws. A Neta cannot rule without his Nari to temper his beast and cubs to lead after him! It was a perfect excuse to get rid of him. Fucking Prince Hunter, the golden boy with his perfect family and life. It should have been mine!"

"Why Blake? Hunter didn't choose his parents any more than you chose yours."

"We're not all perfect princes," he spat the word. "My Dad never stuck around, and my mom was just a human whore like you. She didn't want me. Didn't know what to do with me once I started shifting."

"That's not Hunter's fault. You were his friend. How could you do this?"

Elissa really wanted to know. How could he just plot to betray the only person who had ever shown him any kindness?

"It was easy. I've hated him since I met him," Blake stated.

The truth of his words stung. Her heart ached for her mate. He'd been too kind to this man from the beginning. Accepting him and taking him in. Hunter did not deserve to be treated that way.

Her Tiger's fury on her mate's behalf almost sent her to her knees, but she had to remain vigilant. She wanted to end his life, but even a strong female was no match for a stronger, larger male.

He was once the Beta of the Maverick Pride. However unworthy, he was still a force to be reckoned with. Dammit. She would just have to keep him talking until help arrived.

"Come on, bitch. Enough dallying. It's time for me to remove you from Hunter's life. Now that you're mated, that alone should kill him," he snarled at her.

"Not if I kill you first," she snapped back.

Right then, she could have too. He might be bigger, but he was threatening her heart, her life. No way was Elissa going to take that lying down.

"I'll take it from here, mate."

Elissa turned as Hunter appeared in the doorway. His gold eyes met hers, lips grim, he spoke to her without words conveying his love and anger at the treatment she'd received in under a second. He was making sure she was okay, so she nodded slightly.

That was all he needed. Hunter flew across the room like a raging storm. His fist connected with Blake's face once, twice, hell, she lost count as her mate repeatedly struck.

Blake groaned, then begged, but her mate was beyond pissed. His fury was tangible, and it was right there as he knocked the shit out of the lesser man. Elissa couldn't say she was sorry, especially when Jessica groaned, reminding her Blake had hurt the female.

Protective instincts had her racing to the female's side. Elissa growled when she saw the nasty cut on her scalp from where she'd hit her head on the corner of the countertop.

A crash sounded from the next room, followed by a roar. It sounded as if Blake had hit Hunter over the head with one of the heavy flower vases she had ordered and filled with fall branches and leaves earlier that morning.

The jerk!

She ran to see what was happening, and saw Blake, the coward, using her mate's distraction to his own advantage. Calling on his fur, he meant to attack in his Tiger form!

"Hunter!" she screamed.

But Elissa needn't have bothered. True, a shifted

Blake was running at Hunter with his claws extended, but her mate was one hundred percent Alpha male.

In the blink of an eye, he transformed into his enormous Bengal Tiger. His thick, orange fur had massive black stripes, so dense and glossy, his appearance that much more striking than the ex-Beta. Hunter's beast was easily half again as big as the other man's, with thick muscles and enormous claws and fangs.

He looked more like a prehistoric version of his wild cousins than the muted creature Blake had turned into. Elissa's own beast chuffed in appreciation of his fine figure and his fighting prowess. She could not wait to see him in action.

Bloodthirsty beast, she thought.

The other man tried to fake him out, but Blake grossly underestimated Hunter's speed and strength. One thing was obvious. Her mate's Tiger was done playing.

Elissa knelt beside Jess, having moved her towards the doorway so she could watch the events unfolding. She had a cloth against the other woman's wound and held it there to stem the bleeding.

She was torn between helping her Pride mate and watching the battle. Hunter was her entire life.

Should anything happen, no, it did not bear thinking about!

Luckily, she did not have to ponder it for long. With a tremendous roar, her mate tore Blake's throat out and spat it onto the living room floor like so much garbage. He wasn't wrong, her Tiger insisted.

The smaller Tiger's body twitched and shook as his life drained away. Elissa waited to feel the disgust and regret that she was sure would fill her after such a seemingly senseless death, but she didn't.

In fact, her Tiger roared in approval. The she-beast wanted to bathe in the blood of their enemy.

Okay, well, too bad.

She was so not doing that. Instead, she waited for her mate to stop his snarling to look at her. The Tiger turned his golden gaze, and she found a question there in his eyes.

"You did good. You protected your Nari, now, I need Hunter back," she said, running her hand over the Tiger's head, allowing him to sniff and chuff at her before he shifted back into his human self.

"Elissa," he said, and dropped to his knees.

That brought his head to eye level with her chest. He hesitated for a second. Oh no. She wasn't having that. So, she pounced and brought them both crashing to the floor. His arms engulfed her, crushing her body to his, and she sighed. Much better now.

"Are you alright?"

"Yes. I am fine. Jess, you good?"

"Yeah, yeah. Guess I'll take my lunch to go if y'all are gonna be at each other again," she scrunched her nose, and Elissa couldn't stifle her laugh.

"Oh, hush. We'll eat together. Hunter, put on some clothes," she smiled, and slapped her mate as he growled at his sister.

"Quit it. She stays, and we are gonna eat with our clothes on."

"Uh, Neta?"

Brayden ran in and stopped at the sight that greeted his eyes.

The big man tilted his head and surveyed the room. His eyes bled to black as they rested on Jessica. Then he was crossing the room and hauling the fiery redhead to her feet, checking her over for injury.

"I'm okay," she said quickly, and turned around when her brother stood up.

"*Ewww!* Hunter, put that thing away, for fuck's sake."

"Brayden."

Hunter narrowed his eyes at the big man and cocked his head towards the mess in the hall.

"Call the cleaner. Get this waste out of my house. I want every inch of the hallway cleaned and repainted. And stop fucking touching my sister."

"Yes, Neta," Brayden's voice was deep with his Bear, but he listened to Hunter.

He was a good and loyal Bear. Elissa's Tiger approved, but now she wanted to feed and care for her mate.

"Hunter, go wash up and get dressed," she said, and nuzzled his neck, rubbing her scent on him as she did so.

That was something her cat couldn't seem to get enough of. She always wanted Elissa to press her skin against his, to mark him in that way even though he bore several scratches and bite marks, including the claiming scar she'd given him the day she'd experienced the Puspa.

Sigh.

Elissa had certainly come a long way since the first time she'd seen this man. He'd changed her life, and with each new day came a stronger sense of who she was. This was truly her fate, and she loved him so much for showing her just where she belonged in this world.

With him. Together. Always.

Elissa shooed Hunter along, and he allowed it. For now, but she could tell by the look in his eye he wasn't finished checking on her yet.

The Tiger would want to claim her as soon as they were alone. To celebrate the fact they both still breathed and to reconnect with her on the most basic and yet profound level.

He'd been teaching her about Shifters, and she had to say, they were a damn interesting species. She loved the way he was with her. So honest and true. And she loved belonging to him. He was her family now, and just when she thought she was all alone in the world.

I am definitely lucky, she thought, watching him as he walked over to the bathroom down the hall. He left the door open as he climbed into the shower and rinsed off the blood.

In under three minutes, he was back at her side, dressed in a pair of clean sweats. They kept a pair stashed in just about every room of the house. Another one of those Shifter things.

And Elissa didn't mind it. Not one bit.

Epilogue

Thanksgiving was a big to do now that the Maverick Pride Neta had a Nari at his side. The tantalizing aromas of his mate's expert cooking permeated every nook and cranny of the Pride House.

Hell.

The scents probably filled the whole damn town.

Lucky town.

Elissa had been prepping and cooking for what seemed like days. Rosemary potatoes, sage stuffing, bacon wrapped turkey, pearl onions, honey ham, sweet potato pies, Brussel sprouts roasted with thick slabs of bacon, and more appetizers and sides than he could name.

Finally, with several tables strewn together and a

huge buffet on one end of the enormous dining room, he watched Elissa as she placed the last bowl full of homemade cranberry sauce on the linen cloth. His Nari turned her sight on him unerringly, despite the crowded room, and smiled.

"Everything looks and smells amazing, Lissa," Jess said, echoing his thoughts.

Elissa turned, stretching her back and smiling at the same time. Hunter couldn't wait. He stalked his mate across the room. The rest of the Pride would still be filing in within the next few minutes. The turkeys were resting in the kitchen, and everything else was ready.

In a few minutes, she would want him to help move the ten birds she'd prepared to the mobile carving station she'd had one of the men make her for large dinners just like this.

Being in construction was definitely a plus when it came to his sweet mate's tastes. She was always thinking of ways to improve things in the Pride house, and he was happy to oblige. Hell, he was simply happy to make her happy. Elissa's joy was better than sunshine. Being able to provide whatever it was she wanted was his pleasure.

Figuratively and literally.

This truly was the best Thanksgiving ever.

C.D. GORRI

Hunter had a mate, a true Nari, and his Pride was complete. Plus, he couldn't wait to feast on the delicious meal she'd prepared.

Yum.

Then afterwards, he could feast on her.

Double yum.

This Neta was more than ready to start the celebration.

"You outdid yourself, baby."

"Thank you," she smiled at him.

He walked her backward to the blissfully empty hall, and grabbed his mate by the waist, hauling her against him.

The need to touch her was always there. His skin constantly itched and ached for her.

Only her.

Mine.

He leaned down and captured her lips with his. Like always, the kiss left them both breathless and needy. He scented the dampness that pooled and seeped into her panties as she moaned and tangled her tongue against his.

Clad in another pair of those comfortable jeans and white tank from Jessica's boutique, he was thankful the Pride was so casual about holidays.

It was difficult to get dressed up when the bunch

of them would usually wind up rough-housing and shifting before the night was through.

There was also the bonus that he fucking loved the way she looked like this. Her curves on perfect display for him.

Confident.

Comfortable.

All woman.

My woman.

One large hand cupped her ass while the other snaked around to lift her legs until she was completely off the ground, circling his waist. He liked her like that. Found himself fucking her against walls every chance he got.

Mine.

He licked and kissed her neck and collarbone until he snagged her shirt with his teeth and threatened to tear the fabric to reveal her plump breasts beneath.

It was so fucking hot when she moaned and gave in. Although, every time he did tear a shirt, she reminded him she had few to no actual shirts left.

Fuck it. He'd order her a fucking truckload.

Later.

Oh yeah.

She was going to let him have this one too. He

knew her sighs, recognized her submission as he stroked her cloth covered pussy with his thick shaft. It was exquisite torture. One he didn't want to stop. Fuck no. When he stroked her just right, his kitten purred for him.

Just. Like. That.

Before she could moan his name, the sound of the doorbell rang, and broke them apart.

"Later, I promise," he growled and nipped her lip, bruising but not breaking the sensitive flesh.

"Mine," she purred.

"Yours," he agreed.

The sound of a familiar voice greeted them. Hunter and Elissa turned to see a very special guest had decided to drop by, after all. The Neta and Nari of the Maverick Pride smiled widely and ran to greet him.

"Hello, dear!" Uncle Uzzi took Elissa's hand and gripped it in both of his.

The affectionate squeeze for the old Witch warmed her heart.

"Uncle Uzzi!" she yelled, giving him a quick hug.

Then it was Hunter's turn. The Witch eyed him carefully extracting himself from his mate's arms, but instead of accepting the proffered hand, Hunter shocked them both. He grabbed the old Witch in a back-breaking hug and patted him on the back.

"I owe you everything and more, Uncle Uzzi," Hunter said.

"Well then, maybe you won't mind releasing me so we can salvage the pastries!"

Hunter let go and laughed as the elderly Witch frowned down at the enormous, and currently crumpled, box of delicious smelling pastries from *The Bear Claw Bakery*.

Uh oh.

"No matter," the Witch said, whispering a few words.

Suddenly, the box popped back to its rightful shape and Uzzi handed it to Hunter. He recognized it as a well-known Shifter run establishment.

"Uh, sorry, Uncle Uzzi," Hunter mumbled, placing the box on the dessert table.

"Well, I have to admit I was surprised by your invitation! But I am happy to be here. Elissa, something smells wonderful. Now, how are things?"

"It does, doesn't it? Thank you, everything is great," Hunter said and nodded as Pride members began pouring in.

He noticed a few eyeing the infamous owner of the Magical Matchmaking Service, and he sighed.

He imagined there would be many more mated pairs in the coming years if the elderly Witch had anything to do with it.

And won't that be amazing, insisted his Tiger. *Mated pairs and cubs mean a larger, stronger, happier Pride.*

The animal was correct. His beast chuffed and growled happily. After all, his own mate was carrying their young. Her condition revealed itself the day he'd ended his former Beta's miserable life. Elissa's scent was now permanently mixed with his, but there had been something new then. The fresh new scent had grown stronger until he recognized it as their young.

His chest swelled with pride at the thought. Elissa was everything to him. His Nari. His fated mate. His heart. His entire world.

Her eyes caught his as she greeted their Pride and introduced Uncle Uzzi to his inner circle. Some of the men squirmed, while others seemed interested in getting to know the white-haired Witch.

"Hey," Elissa nuzzled his neck, and he turned his head, allowing the action he knew she loved.

"Hey yourself," he smiled. "Need any help bringing the birds in?"

"Nah, Reg has it. He feels so bad after everything

that happened, he's been my personal slave all week. He'll do anything I say."

That made Hunter's eyes narrow, and Elissa snorted out a laugh.

"Not like that, silly cat. You are my mate, just you," she said and rubbed her cheek on his chest.

His Tiger chuffed inside him.

Reg.

Grrr.

His Tiger still wanted to take a bite out of the young idiot. The male had been sympathetic to Blake in the beginning when his ex-Beta had tried using old Pride laws to sway some of them to his way of thinking.

After being questioned by the Council and by Hunter himself, he found nothing but sincerity and loyalty in the Tiger. Hunter had agreed that if Elissa allowed it, Reg could remain within the Pride.

After asking her, his mate had been willing to accept his apology. Even more, she'd requested he be assigned to her, and his Honor Guard duties resumed.

Along with a few additional guards whenever he was out, Hunter had reluctantly agreed. Oh yes, she was something, his little Nari.

"What are you thinking?" she asked.

"Besides how much I love you?"

"Yes," she said, smiling like he knew she would. "Besides that."

"I was thinking that things are going to get interesting around here if anyone else decides to take Uncle Uzzi up on his offer to help them find their mates."

"Yes, it will," Elissa said and laughed.

"I wonder if anyone will wind up as *purrfectly mated* as we are."

At that, Hunter joined her in laughing out loud, earning them a couple of curious stares from their Pride mates.

"I love you," he said, and kissed her again.

"Did I mention I want pie for dessert?"

"Do you now?"

"Yes. My favorite flavor, with cream," he whispered naughtily. His chest rumbled with his Tiger, and fuck, his mouth watered a little.

"It's all yours, mate," she said, kissing him back and making his Tiger purr with need.

"Love you, my Nari."

Prrrrrrrrrrrrrrrrrrrrrrrrrrr.

. . .

The end.

Thank you so much for reading! Did you enjoy this story about a growly Tiger Shifter and his perfectly curvy human mate? Want more Maverick Pride Tales?

Click here.

A Note From the Author

Hello readers!

Thanks so much for grabbing my newly updated Maverick Pride Tale book! If it seems familiar, this series was previously part of a shared world. I've added almost 20,000 words to book 1, with new cover art, new characters, and plot twists, and a run through by my favorite editing team, to enhance your reading enjoyment.

I really hope you liked it.

You can stay tuned for more of my books, including sneak peeks at even more Maverick Pride Tales, by signing up for my newsletter here.

You can also look forward to a completely revamped Dire Wolf Mates and Wyvern Protection Unit series coming soon!

A NOTE FROM THE AUTHOR

Thanks again.
Del mare alla stella,
C.D. Gorri

P.S.

Don't forget to tell me how you liked this story by leaving your honest review.

No pressure.

A review can be one or two brief sentences where you simply state whether you enjoyed the story and would recommend it to someone! It is an enormous help to authors and the best way for us to reach larger audiences so we can keep writing the stories you love.

Have you met my Bears?

Looking for a Paranormal Romance series that is loads of growly fun?

Meet the Barvale Clan first in the Bear Claw Tales! A complete shifter romance series about 4 brothers who discover and need to win their fated mates!

Followed by two more spin off series, the Barvale Clan Tales and the Barvale Holiday Tales!

No cliffhangers. Steamy PNR fun. Go and read your next happily ever after today!

Beware... Here Be Dragons!

The Falk Clan Tales began as my stories surrounding four dragon Brothers and how they find their one true mates, but when a long lost brother arrives on the scene, followed by a few more Shifters...what can I say? The more the merrier!

Each Dragon's chest is marked with his rose, the magical link to his heart and his magic. They each have a matching gemstone to go with it.

She's given up on love, but he's just begun.

In *The Dragon's Valentine* we meet the eldest Falk brother, Callius. He is on a mission to find a Castle and his one true mate, one he can trust with his diamond rose....

His heart is frozen; can she change his mind about love?

In *The Dragon's Christmas Gift* our attention shifts to Alexsander, the youngest brother of the four. He has resigned himself to a life alone, until he meets *her*.

Some wounds run deep, can a Dragon's heart be unbroken?

The Dragon's Heart is the story of Edric Falk who has vowed never to love again, but that changes when he meets his feisty mate, Joselyn Curacao.

She just wants a little fun, he's looking for a lifetime.

We finally meet Nikolai Falk and his sexy Shifter mate in *The Dragon's Secret*.

*Now available in a boxed set.

Guess what…. I've got more Dragons on the way!

Look for The Dragon's Treasure now available where ebooks are sold!

The Dragon's Dream and The Dragon's Surprise are coming soon!

Other Titles by C.D. Gorri

Young Adult Urban Fantasy Books:

Wolf Moon: A Grazi Kelly Novel Book 1

Hunter Moon: A Grazi Kelly Novel Book 2

Rebel Moon: A Grazi Kelly Novel Book 3

Winter Moon: A Grazi Kelly Novel Book 4

Chasing The Moon: A Grazi Kelly Short 5

Blood Moon: A Grazi Kelly Novel 6

*Get all 6 books NOW AVAILABLE IN A BOXED SET:

The Complete Grazi Kelly Novel Series

Casting Magic: The Angela Tanner Files 1

Keeping Magic: The Angela Tanner Files 2

G'Witches Magical Mysteries Series

Co-written with P. Mattern

G'Witches

G'Witches 2: The Hary Harbinger

<u>Paranormal Romance Books:</u>

<u>Macconwood Pack Novel Series:</u>

Charley's Christmas Wolf: A Macconwood Pack Novel 1

Cat's Howl: A Macconwood Pack Novel 2

Code Wolf: A Macconwood Pack Novel 3

The Witch and The Werewolf: A Macconwood Pack Novel 4

To Claim a Wolf: A Macconwood Pack Novel 5

Conall's Mate: A Macconwood Pack Novel 6

Her Solstice Wolf: A Macconwood Pack Novel 7

Werewolf Fever: A Macconwood Pack Novel 8

Also available in 2 boxed sets:

The Macconwood Pack Volume 1

The Macconwood Pack Volume 2

<u>Macconwood Pack Tales Series:</u>

Wolf Bride: The Story of Ailis and Eoghan A Macconwood Pack Tale 1

Summer Bite: A Macconwood Pack Tale 2

His Winter Mate: A Macconwood Pack Tale 3

Snow Angel: A Macconwood Pack Tale 4

Charley's Baby Surprise: A Macconwood Pack Tale 5

Home for the Howlidays: A Macconwood Pack Tale 6

A Silver Wedding: A Macconwood Pack Tale 7

Mine Furever: A Macconwood Pack Tale 8

A Furry Little Christmas: A Macconwood Pack Tale 9

Also available in two boxed sets:

The Macconwood Pack Tales Volume 1

Shifters Furever: The Macconwood Pack Tales Volume 2

<u>*The Falk Clan Tales:*</u>

The Dragon's Valentine: A Falk Clan Novel 1

The Dragon's Christmas Gift: A Falk Clan Novel 2

The Dragon's Heart: A Falk Clan Novel 3

The Dragon's Secret: A Falk Clan Novel 4

The Dragon's Treasure: A Falk Clan Novel 5

Dragon Mates: The Falk Clan Series Boxed Set Books 1-4

<u>*The Bear Claw Tales:*</u>

Bearly Breathing: A Bear Claw Tale 1

Bearly There: A Bear Claw Tale 2

Bearly Tamed: A Bear Claw Tale 3

Bearly Mated: A Bear Claw Tale 4

Also available in a boxed set:

The Complete Bear Claw Tales (Books 1-4)

<u>*The Barvale Clan Tales:*</u>

Polar Opposites: The Barvale Clan Tales 1

Polar Outbreak: The Barvale Clan Tales 2

Polar Compound: A Barvale Clan Tale 3

Polar Curve: A Barvale Clan Tale 4

Also available in a boxed set:

The Barvale Clan Tales (Books 1-4)

<u>*Barvale Holiday Tales:*</u>

A Bear For Christmas

Hers To Bear

Thank You Beary Much

Also available in a boxed set:

The Barvale Holiday Tales (Books 1-3)

<u>*Purely Paranormal Pleasures:*</u>

Marked by the Devil: Purely Paranormal Pleasures

Mated to the Dragon King: Purely Paranormal Pleasures

Claimed by the Demon: Purely Paranormal Pleasures

Christmas with a Devil, a Dragon King, & a Demon: Purely Paranormal Pleasures (short story)

Vampire Lover: Purely Paranormal Pleasures

Grizzly Lover: Purely Paranormal Pleasures

Elvish Lover: Purely Paranormal Pleasures

Hot Dire Wolf Nights: Purely Paranormal Pleasures

Christmas With Her Chupacabra: Purely Paranormal Pleasures

<u>The Wardens of Terra:</u>

Bound by Air: The Wardens of Terra Book 1

Star Kissed: A Wardens of Terra Short

Waterlocked: The Wardens of Terra Book 2

Moon Kissed: A Wardens of Terra Short

*Now in a boxed set and in audio!

<u>The Maverick Pride Tales:</u>

SERIES MAKEOVER COMING SOON

<u>Dire Wolf Mates:</u>

SERIES MAKEOVER COMING SOON

<u>Wyvern Protection Unit:</u>

SERIES MAKEOVER COMING SOON

<u>Standalones:</u>

The Enforcer

Blood Song: A Sanguinem Council Book

<u>EveL Worlds:</u>

Chinchilla and the Devil: A FUCN'A Book

Sammi and the Jersey Bull: A FUCN'A Book

Mouse and the Ball: A FUCN'A Book

<u>The Guardians of Chaos:</u>

Wolf Shield: Guardians of Chaos Book 1

Dragon Shield: Guardians of Chaos Book 2

Stallion Shield: Guardians of Chaos Book 3

Panther Shield: Guardians of Chaos 4

Witch Shield: Guardians of Chaos 5

Howl's Romance

Mated to the Werewolf Next Door: A Howl's Romance

The Tiger King's Christmas Bride

Claiming His Virgin Mate: Howls Romance

Twice Mated Tales

Doubly Claimed

Doubly Bound

Doubly Tied

Hearts of Stone Series

Shifter Mountain: Hearts of Stone 1

Shifter City: Hearts of Stone 2

Shifter Village: Hearts of Stone 3

Accidentally Undead Series

Fangs For Nothin'

Moongate Island Tales

Moongate Island Mate

Mated in Hope Falls

Mated by Moonlight

Speed Dating with the Denizens of the Underworld

Ash: Speed Dating with the Denizens of Underworld

Arachne: Speed Dating with the Denizens of Underworld

<u>Hungry Fur Love</u>

Hungry Like Her Wolf: Magic and Mayhem Universe

<u>Shifters Unleashed Boxed Sets</u>

Check out these amazing anthologies where you can find some of my books and the works of other awesome authors!

Midnight Magic Anthology (Water Witch)

Rituals & Runes Anthology (Air Witch)

<u>Island Stripe Pride</u>

Tiger Claimed

<u>NYC Shifter Tales</u>

Cuff Linked

Sealed Fate

<u>A Howlin' Good Fairytale Retelling</u>

Sweet As Candy (as seen in Once Upon An Ever After)

<u>Coming Soon:</u>

If The Shoe Fits: A Howlin' Good Fairytale Retelling

Spring Fling (co-written with P. Mattern)

For Fangs Sake

Tiger Denied

Moongate Island Captive

Hungry For Her Bear: Magic and Mayhem Universe

The Dragon's Surprise

The Dragon's Dream

Bearing Gifts

Taming Magic: The Angela Tanner Files 3

Vampire Shield: Guardians of Chaos 6

Chickee and the Paparazzi: FUCN'A

The Wolf's Winter Wish: A Macconwood Pack Tale

The Hybrid Assassin

Excerpt from Wolf Shield: Guardians of Chaos by C.D. Gorri

What a day! Fergie McAndrews headed towards the pick-up truck she'd borrowed from her roommate for work that morning.

Of course, the thirty-thousand dollar certified used luxury car she'd splurged on earlier in the year was in the shop. Again.

Just another in a long line of bad decisions. After leaving a perfectly good job for a startup company, she was laid off three weeks ago and had to borrow money from her parents to pay rent. Wasn't that humiliating?

"This is the last time, Ferg," her step-monster had said *after she'd Venmo'd the money to her.*

God forbid the mechanic call and tell her the car

was ready. She wouldn't be able to pick it up for another week. That was when she got her first paycheck from her newest gig at L-Corp. Not a startup, but an older company with new offices in Bayonne, which was only a half-hour commute.

But to commute, you needed a car. Fergie had no choice but to borrow the old pick-up from her best friend and roommate, Jessenia Banks. It wasn't like she needed the truck. She worked from home these days. Besides, Fergie promised to fill it up and have it washed.

She huffed out a breath. It'd been a really long day. A crappy one too. Fergie wanted to love her new job. Really, she did. But so far, it was the pits. If Fergie wanted to be a librarian, she would've been one.

Research was her jam. Well, when it was interesting. She had a knack for sniffing out information and compiling easy-to-read spreadsheets and timelines. It wasn't the hard work that annoyed her. Her complaint was the content. The actual stuff her new boss had her looking up. It was beyond boring.

Why an enormous conglomerate like L-Corp needed old land surveys, cross-referenced with newspaper reports on accidents, crimes, etcetera.

EXCERPT FROM WOLF SHIELD: GUARDIANS OF CHAOS B...

She had no idea. She'd been at it for weeks now. So far, she'd researched six locations given via GPS coordinates across Hudson County. Her new boss wanted everything, every little insignificant piece of information she could dig up.

That was the easy part. It was the hassle of the actual job that really made her want to give up. Every day she had to drive to Bayonne to pick up her work laptop she'd dropped off the night before with all of that day's findings. Every single night they wiped her computer clean.

Like she was going to run away with the secrets of what happened on 2nd and Washington sixty-years ago. Can you say paranoid? Ugh.

Fergie had always looked forward to working for a huge global company. It was supposed to be her ticket out of the Garden State. Traveling the globe, seeing new things, visiting far-off places was always a secret dream of hers. Well, that, and having her own walk-in closet full of gorgeous designer shoes.

Best secret dream evah! In her opinion, anyway. What woman didn't love shoes? Fergie hummed as she daydreamed about rows and rows of Blahnik's, Jimmy Choo's, Garavani's, Ferragamo's, and her personal favorites, Louboutin's on every shelf!

Don't judge. Fergie wasn't shallow, she just liked pretty things. Haters gonna hate. But every time she ran across a thrift or second-chance store, she'd search high and low to see what they had. That was how she'd scored the pumps on her feet.

They made her feel good about herself. Being five-foot two-inches short with more curves than a racetrack, Fergie had had more than her fair share of self-esteem issues growing up. Alright, so she was chubby. She could admit that proudly now.

If everyone looked the same, the world would be one boring as hell place. Fergie liked herself perfectly fine these days, in spite of all the times her step-monster tried to make her diet growing up. So she liked food and shoes. Big deal.

She worked hard to feed and clothe herself, so as far as she was concerned, no one had a right to comment. So what if she wanted some excitement in her life? Fergie was aware she was better off than most, but what was wrong with having goals?

She'd spent a lot of time thinking about how a woman like her could have an adventure. Travelling was the only thing she could think of. Of course, she'd been hoping this job would be the answer to that. Even travelling for work was better than being stuck.

Sigh.

So far, her plans had fallen flat, but hey, at least she was earning a paycheck. Her new boss, Mr. Offner, might be a strange man, but he signed her checks, and that was enough for now. Fergie had never seen more than a glimpse of him. All of her instructions usually came via email.

Most of the time she was able to compile her research quickly, then she'd head back to the office to organize it into neat little spreadsheets, and finally, she'd hand it all in with her laptop. But not today.

Mr. Offner sent her an email detailing everything she could dig up on one of the oldest places on record in the county. Of course, land surveys that old, along with police reports, newspaper articles, deeds, and sales records were nowhere she could easily access them.

After wasting hours at both the court house and municipal building, Fergie had been directed to the *second* public library. Apparently anything over a hundred years old was filed away in the godforsaken place. She'd been shocked to find an entire room filled with musty old archives. And wouldn't you know it, there was no cell service and no internet access. Plus, their phone lines were down. She'd had to photograph each page using her cell. When she got home later, she would send those photos like a fax to her boss along with her spreadsheet. If she could manage that before collapsing into bed.

Excerpt from *Bound by Air* by C.D. Gorri

Troy Waman looked down at his smartphone to the little red arrow blinking on his map app, indicating he had reached his destination. He frowned pensively before shaking his head.

"What a fucking shithole," he murmured to himself as he exited the nondescript black SUV his Station Master, Rex, had given him for the job.

"Try not to scratch it," the tough Bear shifter had said with a barely contained growl after their meeting the day before last. After a thousand years of waiting, The *Wardens of Terra* were being called to duty and this was Troy's first assignment.

It took him a day and a half to make his way to Shadowland, New York from the little suburb in Virginia Beach where his Station was located. There were dozens of them across the continental United States and even more overseas, though he'd rarely been out of the county himself.

Troy rolled his shoulders and exhaled. He was the first from his Station to be called to duty. A fact that left him both proud and humbled at the same time. He'd trained damn hard since he was a child waiting for such an opportunity. Now he had it, and it was almost too much to bear.

Fuck and damn. It's time Troy, get your ass in gear. That was all the sympathy he had for himself. Why the hell should he have any at all? Troy Waman was no tenderfoot normal. He was a Warden of Terra. He didn't need to remind himself of the honor and duty that went along with his position.

The *Wardens of Terra* were an ancient group of elite warriors. All of them Shifters. Identified in their youth and trained throughout their preternaturally long lives, they were guardians as well as fighters. *Station Masters* led teams of Wardens across the planet.

Though they'd been deactivated sometime in the last millennium, Wardens were born, chosen, and trained every day with the distinct knowledge that someday, they'd be called upon to defend the earth. That day was here.

Troy Waman had been trained as a Warden since before he learned how to spell the word. His heritage was a mix of Anglo and Native American. His father's blood was a mix of tribes including Algonquin, Lenape, Cherokee, and a few others. He hadn't stuck around long enough for anyone to learn the rest.

He supposed he could get a DNA test, but that might raise too many questions with the normals. Especially in this day of advanced technology in biogenetics.

Besides, it was quite common in today's world to find Native American peoples descended from multiple tribes. Troy Waman was uncommon for an entirely different reason. He was a Shifter, a special race of dual natured beings with one foot in the supernatural world and one in the human. Troy was a *Thunderbird Shifter* to be exact. Something unique even amongst Shifters.

He stretched his long, lithe body as he stepped away from the vehicle. It was already dark out despite it being fairly early in the evening. *Daylight savings my ass.* He sniffed the frigid air. The unusually high winds made the cold seem even more bitter. The street lamp stuttered on the corner, a rusty fence squeaked, and a black cat crossed the street, ducking under some parked cars. Troy's frown deepened.

It looked like the setting of a B-horror flick. All it needed was some half naked co-ed to run down the street with a masked bogeyman stalking behind her, traditional blood-coated knife in hand. *Oh yeah.* They might call it *Shadowland Nightmare* or something equally cheesy.

He stopped his musings and used his heightened senses to take in the downtrodden area around him. It would seem upstate New York wasn't all orchards and sprawling suburbs. He smirked as the "I love New York" song ran through his head. *Yeah, right.*

Apparently, parts of the Empire State were as fucked up as the street where he was born in Newark, New Jersey. He'd visited that shithole back when he was in his teens just out of curiosity. What a mistake that had been! He'd left almost as soon as he'd arrived. His extended family had been, shall we say, less than welcoming.

His gray-haired grandmother had screamed and crossed herself when he stepped over her threshold. He was what they called a *skin walker*. They feared and loathed him as something evil. Him evil? Like he was the motherfucker who knocked-up some unsuspecting normal and left her ass with a Shifter baby.

He was not evil, but he was something they did not understand. He'd been angry and ashamed that day. He'd crashed through his grandmother's kitchen to hitch a ride back down to his Station in Virginia Beach.

In his youth it was more like a military training camp, but it was all he knew of home. After all, it was where he'd lived his entire life. He'd made his peace and settled fully into his life there.

The incident with his grandmother had happened over a decade ago, when Troy had stolen his records out of Rex's office. Still, the memory remained fresh in his mind as if it were only yesterday. The fucked-up street where he was standing only brought back the painful reminder that he'd come from the same kind of squalor. *Fuck this*, he thought.

The pungent scent of despair washed over him. *Reminding him.* A young man with a hood pulled up over his head, eyed him from the street corner. *Drug dealer. Shadowland* indeed. It was an apt name for this shamble of a neighborhood.

The young man continued to stare until Troy allowed his beast to shine through. His golden eyes pinned the errant youth through the inky darkness of the night. Startled, the kid dropped the bag he was holding and ran down the alley.

Punk. Troy walked over and picked up what he had so hastily left behind. A couple of grams of crack cocaine and heroin, *probably cut with Fentanyl.* There were also various sized baggies full of what smelled like some below average marijuana and half-rotted psychedelic mushrooms.

Just your garden variety of illegal substances to be found on most street corners in neighborhoods like this one. *Fucking normals.* He frowned and dumped the still sealed contents down the closest storm drain. He sent a quick text to Rex earmarking the location.

Rex would make sure the local police department got an anonymous tip to retrieve the narcotics before someone got hurt. Recreational drug use, mainly the opioid epidemic, was wreaking havoc amongst the humans with more and more of them succumbing to their addictions.

It was troubling, but not Troy's problem. Shifters were extraordinarily hard to kill. Most human drugs had little to no effect on supernatural beings. *Normals,* he growled the thought, *such weak creatures.*

To be fair, Shifters had vices too. He just had little

experience with it. Cecil, a Station-mate of his, had an adrenaline addiction. He was always putting himself in dangerous situations, even during simple training exercises. Fernandez, a Jaguar Shifter, was always trying to get into some chick's pants. *Sex addict.* And he knew of others who channeled their energies into ways he considered to be mostly unproductive.

His opinion, for sure. He'd always been something of a loner by nature. There weren't many Thunderbird Shifters around. Hell, he was the only fucking one he knew of in this part of the world.

He didn't blame or judge his Station-mates for their proclivities. Most of the Shifters he knew had large appetites which included food, exercise, and sex.

Troy had certainly explored that part of him. He wasn't a man-whore or anything, but he'd had his share of women. None of them mattered to him. Just a means to satisfy the occasional itch.

Troy was determined to live his life as a Warden of Terra alone. He never expected to find anyone willing to share what was a potentially deadly existence.

Those who followed the Darkness and evil were always looking for ways to gain the upper hand and it was his job to stop them. The way he saw it, it was an honor and a duty to serve.

He shared this great responsibility with the entire organization. The core belief of the Wardens was based on one indisputable fact Shifters had walked the earth since the dawn of time, even before humankind; therefore, they were responsible for the well-being of the entire planet and all its inhabitants. Especially those who were inherently weaker. Mainly females and *normals*.

There were other supernaturals who believed humans, or normals as they referred to them, were a blight on the planet. Those creatures wished to destroy them and take over.

Demons, Dark Witches, and a whole plethora of evil beings sought the destruction of the normals and the world they lived in. *Idiots! Did they even realize if they destroyed the world, there would be nothing left? Where the fuck would they live?*

Of course, the supernatural world had many agencies that worked towards the common goal of saving the planet. The *Order of the Guardians,* for example, were responsible for policing the various factions of supernaturals.

Shifters generally tended to ally themselves with the Guardians. Sure, there were *bad* Shifters, but he'd never come across any willing to follow the Dark. Simply because most agreed the destruction of the world could not be allowed to happen.

Different Packs and Clans, etcetera, of course, had different ideas. Some wanted to remain secret, others wished to come out, and other still wanted to rule the weaker humans. It was a whole fucking thing, and they argued about regularly.

Troy didn't know from any of that. He spent little time in the human world. His efforts better spent making himself worthy of being a Warden. Training, exercise, and following orders. That's what Troy lived for, it was why he was chosen.

Thunderbird Shifters were very rare. *Special*. He scoffed at the stray thought. But no matter what way he looked at it, Troy was indeed unique. In more ways than one. He was born *marked* by the stars. A *Shifter of Terra*.

From infancy, he was told he carried the power of his sign within him. *Aquarius* ruled his destiny and it would aid him in the never-ending battle against the forces of darkness.

Every single Warden he knew was a Shifter like him. They were the fiercest warriors on the planet. Like many others throughout the last thousand years, Troy, *a Shifter child who was marked*, was taken

EXCERPT FROM BOUND BY AIR BY C.D. GORRI

from his parents and trained by his Station Master until the time when he would be called into use.

All that time, he thought, *and here I am*. He tried to ignore the pressure building inside of him. He felt anxious. His animal pressed against his psyche, comforting him with his presence.

The significance of the moment was not lost on him. The Wardens had waited a millennium to be called to act. *He* had been waiting his entire life.

"Do not fear the future, Troy," the Herald who had visited his Station said to him when he'd brought word that they had been activated, *"Your destiny awaits."*

Troy wondered if the old man referred to the Wardens finally being called to act, or if the elder spoke of yet another legend. Troy had been shocked to say the least when the Herald had entered their tidy little Station in Virginia Beach with his flowing white hair. After he told them the news, he turned to Troy and recited another old tale.

"Young Thunderbird, you are the first to return us to Terra. Do not doubt your worth. Your destiny has been written in the stars since before you were born, Troy Waman. Remember, a Warden discovers his true measure when his fated mate is thrust upon him."

Whatever the fuck that meant. Troy looked down at

his phone, then to the street sign on the corner, and finally, to the faded numbers painted on the mailbox in front of the ramble of a house his map app had brought him to.

Fuck, am I thinking? Fated mates are myths. Stories made up so orphaned Shifters would sleep through the night. He scoffed at the thought. Memories of tales the head nurse, Sr. Maria, had told him at the training camp he'd called home for years invaded his brain.

Memories were pesky things. Sometimes eternal, and always fucking portable. But he was no longer a child. *No more stories, Sister. Now, I act.*

"A thousand years we've waited, and I'm walking into a fucking scene from a bad episode of *Hoarders*," Troy shook his head and frowned at the decrepit house that sat a few hundred feet away from him.

It was cold as fuck outside and his leather jacket did little to warm him. Avian Shifters did not carry around the same bulk as other types of Shifters. He ran hotter than normals, but the single digit temperature froze him to the bone.

True, he wasn't beefy like some of his fellow Shifters, but he was just as incredibly strong, and he was wicked fast. Much stronger than any average male. He paused briefly gauging the atmosphere.

EXCERPT FROM BOUND BY AIR BY C.D. GORRI

There was something off about the place. He scented *Magic* and something else. His Bird bristled beneath his skin. *Easy now.*

Lightning flashed in the darkened skies, allowing him to see the worn shingles, and cracked siding of the beaten-up colonial in greater detail. More than one window had been smashed and boarded up with cheap plywood.

If anything, it enhanced the creepy haunted house feel of the place. The porch sagged dangerously. He wondered how the place had managed to not be condemned by the town. One thing was certain, it was an ugly little turd of a house.

Who the hell put gray siding on their house anyway? Maybe it wasn't always that color. Maybe the owner liked gray. *Whatever.* He couldn't give two shits about the siding.

His only concern was the increased supernatural activity in the area over the past two weeks. Ever since the owner, a *Mrs. Renalda Curosi*, passed away. *A haunting?*

A creaking sound floated up to his ears and he stilled his movements. The sound developed into more of a *moaning* noise. An unearthly wail. It grew louder as the lightning continued to flash in the sky.

Troy had never seen a ghost. True, there were a

lot of things in the universe he had never seen nor heard of, but that didn't make them any less real.

If ghosts were real, and they made noises, he imagined that pitiful wail was damn close to what it would sound like.

No such thing as ghosts. Yeah, well, most people had never heard of Shifters either. And yet, there he stood.

His Thunderbird shifted once more beneath his skin, the beast flexing his senses as the lightning in the air drew him to the surface. *No.* He told his other half. His human needed to be in control now. He walked across the street, keeping to the shadows.

Something was indeed off about the creepy old house. He inched further to the black door. The knocker was in the shape of a face or mask. No discernible features, just a vague impression of eyes, nose, and mouth. *Shadowland indeed.*

He listened with his enhanced hearing and frowned. There was a distinct voice somewhere beneath the moaning and creaking. A *female* voice. His curiosity was piqued.

From what he'd seen in her file, Mrs. Curosi was ninety-seven when she passed. Her closest living relative was a half-sister, a *Magdelena Kristos*, and she lived over three hours away in New Jersey. The half-sister was cut from Mrs. Curosi's will recently. She'd bequeathed her entire estate, house, bank account, and all her earthly belongings, to someone named *A. Kristos. Another sister? Maybe.*

Troy hadn't given it much thought until now. A crash sounded from inside the house. He perked up as the feminine voice he'd thought he'd heard earlier screamed in pain. *Time to act.*

Excerpt from Fangs For Nothin' by C.D. Gorri

"Are you out of your mind?"

Xavier DuMont, Vampire and Prince of the Tenebris Clan out of DuMont, New Jersey, ran a hand over his face. It was almost five in the morning on Wednesday, and he was still going over the weekly requests and complaints.

He could not believe it. One after the other, he'd received dozens of requests for formal introductions for most of the eligible young females in the Clan by their parents or some family matchmaker or other. It was the 21st Century, and yet, the Vampires of the Tenebris Clan still thought he needed an arranged marriage to run things!

"No, Lucius, I assure you my mind is sound."

"How can you be thinking of going away? To some retreat? At this time of year! You know, the whole Clan is up in arms over the tax laws your father had set into motion before his demise. Some are questioning your right to rule. Then, there is still the matter of your mating—"

"Lucius, for the love of fuck! I know what is going on in my own Clan. I am even now revoking those tax laws, people will just have to be patient."

"And what about meeting with these young females? Maybe that will quell some of the unrest—"

"No! I am not inclined to take a mate at this time. My father's grave has barely begun to grow grass. There is no rush!"

"There is pressure though, sire," Lucius Redwing insisted.

He was Xavier's oldest and most reliable friend. At nearly three hundred years old, they'd known each other for a considerable length of time. Lucius had been his childhood companion when they'd fled France for the New World. After settling the town of DuMont, his father had not only been the most productive of the local normals, but he had taken over their branch of the Clan.

Breaking ties with the old regime, and establishing their own rule, the DuMonts had done exceedingly well. Of course, coming into the new century had been difficult for some, but Xavier was determined to do it, to breathe new life into the old-fashioned world of Vampires. He would see them succeed and blossom in this age that was simply exploding with technology.

"I know you have plans, sire. But the anxious mamas are already parading their daughters resumes as if they were applying for a job." Lucius grinned. He waved a manila envelope bursting with applications for audiences with him from the most prestigious Vampire families in all of DuMont.

"For fuck's sake, Luc. Get rid of them," Xavier growled, and ran a hand over his face.

"Now, now. Surely, you know enough not to disrespect tradition and courtesy. These families are your staunchest supporters. Without their aid, your ascension to leadership could be challenged. The right mate would stop all of that—"

"I will not be forced into this, Luc. If anyone wants to challenge me for the right to lead, then he or she can face me out in the open. Not hide behind some political game."

"But sire—"

"No. I will not be manipulated. You should know that of me, old friend."

"Yes. Of course." Lucius nodded, placing the hefty envelope on the corner of Xavier's desk.

Vampires did not always inherit the right to lead. Princes were not born but made. Wasn't that what his father had always said? And yet, royal blood flowed in his veins. And it was because of that blood —*his royal DuMont blood*—that so many hungry mamas yearned to tie one of their young to him for eternity.

Fortunately, Xavier had avoided them. He refused to be pressured to take any of the hungry misses for his mate, as of yet. But with his recent ascension, that pressure was now on full keel.

Shit and fuck.

"I've got an idea," Lucius said, thrusting a copy of *The Nightly News* at him.

"What is it, Luc? I am in no mood."

"Read there," his friend said, pointing at an article on the bottom left.

"A retreat? I haven't been on one of those since I was ninety."

"Yes, but remember the fun? I brought my *sheep* at the time, and you pouted because I wouldn't share her!"